003157

FAIRY TALES OF
HANS CHRISTIAN ANDERSEN

FAIRY TALES OF
HANS CHRISTIAN ANDERSEN

Retold by
SUSAN DICKINSON

Illustrated by
KATE ALDOUS

First published 1993
An Albion Book

Produced exclusively for W H Smith Ltd
1993

Conceived, designed and produced by
The Albion Press Ltd, Spring Hill, Idbury, Oxfordshire OX7 6RU

Designer: Emma Bradford
Copy editor: Elizabeth Wilkes

ISBN 1 871927 03 X

Typesetting by York House Typographic Ltd, London
Colour origination by York House Graphics Ltd, London
Printed and bound in Great Britain by Bath Press Colourbooks Ltd, Glasgow

CONTENTS

ABOUT HANS CHRISTIAN ANDERSEN

Hans Christian Andersen, the most famous and best-loved of all the world's writers for children, was born in Odense, Denmark, on 2 April, 1805. His parents were poor, but loving. His mother was a washerwoman, and his father was a shoemaker.

He remembered his father as "a man of a richly gifted and truly poetical mind," who gave up his Sunday leisure to make toy theatres for his son, or read to him from *The Arabian Nights*. The world of his imagination was further enlarged by the stories told to him by the old women in the spinning-room of the local poor house, where his grandmother tended the garden. He remembered that, when he amused the women with his childish talk, "they rewarded my eloquence by telling me tales in return; and thus a world as rich as that of the *Thousand and One Nights* was revealed to me." These folktales full of humour and wonder became the model on which he was to base his own fairy tales.

The "salt" of humour in Andersen's tales is perhaps his most characteristic feature, and one which early translators disastrously failed to notice. One of these, Mary Howitt, famously assured Charles Dickens that not only was Andersen's English poor, but he couldn't even speak Danish! In fact, his decision to write in the robust, direct language of everyday speech, rather than a high-flown literary style, is what has kept his stories alive.

When Andersen came to write his autobiography, he called it *The Fairy Tale of My Life*. But he had already written his life story as a fairy tale, many times over. The most famous self-portrait of all is that of "The Ugly Duckling," but Andersen's tales are full of glimpses of his life and character.

That character was not an easy one, for Andersen, while he loved company and longed for friendship and approval, was a nervy, worried man – sensitive to every slight, and anxious about every social situation. He remained, in fact, a child in adult company, and like a child tended to show off when he felt ill-at-ease. After he stayed with Charles Dickens in 1857, the English author, scrupulously polite and attentive to his guest throughout his stay, couldn't resist putting up a notice in Andersen's bedroom when he left: "Hans Andersen slept in this room for five weeks – which seemed to the family AGES!"

He was more relaxed with children, and, as Dickens's young son, Henry, remembered: "He had one beautiful accomplishment, which was the cutting out in paper, with an ordinary pair of scissors, of lovely little figures of spirits and elves, gnomes, fairies and animals of all kinds, which might well have stepped out of the pages of his books." Andersen was a talented artist in drawing and collage, but these paper cut-outs were his speciality: favourite subjects included castles, swans, goblins, hearts, and ballet dancers – the characters and settings of stories such as "The Constant Tin Soldier."

Like the constant tin soldier, Andersen always felt the odd one out; and like the constant tin soldier, he had to make his own way in a worrying world.

His father died when he was eleven, and he was briefly apprenticed in a cloth mill and then sent to work in a tobacco factory. But he did not want to be a factory hand or an artisan: he had fallen in love with the theatre, and dreamed of being an actor or singer. He begged his mother to allow him to go to Copenhagen to seek his fortune. He knew, he told her, the pattern of such things: "First you go through terrible suffering, then you become famous." He was buoyed up by the prophecy of a "wise woman" who told him that he would become a great man, and that one day Odense would be illuminated in his honour: a prophecy that came true.

So at the age of fourteen, Andersen set off alone to Copenhagen. There the gawky, odd, dreamy boy suffered both a series of rebuffs to his dreams of fame on the stage and a series of kindnesses from members of the Danish literary and artistic community, who recognized some special quality in him. It was their generosity that secured him an education, and kept him alive.

His theatrical ambitions in tatters, Hans Christian then dreamed of becoming a writer. He began to make a reputation with poems, travel writing, and novels such as *The Improvisatore*, but it was not until the end of 1834 that he began to write his first fairy tales. He showed them to his friend, the famous scientist H. C. Ørsted, and wrote in a letter: "Ørsted says that if *The Improvisatore* will make me famous, the fairy tales will make me immortal."

The first four stories, including "The Princess and the Pea," were published in 1835. He continued to publish small batches of tales until, when the last four came out in 1872, he had written over a hundred and fifty. They were something quite new in literature, and, in them, Hans Christian Andersen found his voice. The uncertain tone of his adult writings gives way to an absolute confidence in his fairy tales. They almost seemed to write themselves. For instance his masterpiece "The Snow Queen," was begun on 5 December 1844; on 21 December, it was not only finished, but printed and published. He wrote to a friend, "It came dancing out over the paper."

Andersen died on 4 August 1875; he had never married, despite several unrequited romantic attachments, for instance to the singer Jenny Lind, for whom he wrote "The Nightingale." He was already famous throughout the world. In many ways a lonely man, he had nevertheless found his own happiness in the enchanted world of his imagination: a world where he could prove, in the compelling and potent images of "The Snow Queen," that love is stronger than death. His fairy tales had, as Ørsted foretold, made him immortal.

THE NIGHTINGALE

In China, a good many years ago, there was an emperor whose palace was made entirely of fine porcelain. In the garden were the most wonderful flowers, to the best of which silver bells were tied, so that nobody passed by without noticing them. And the garden itself was so huge that even the gardener did not know how far it stretched. It was possible to walk on and on until you came to a glorious forest with flowering trees and deep lakes. At the end of the forest there was the sea where ships sailed in beneath the branches of the trees. Among the trees there lived a nightingale which sang so sweetly that even the poor fisherman stopped to listen, although he should have been out at sea casting his nets.

"How beautiful that is!" he would say.

People came from all over the world to the city of the Emperor. Many were invited to the palace and all who came admired it and the wonderful garden. But when they heard the nightingale, they said, "That is the best of all."

When they went home they wrote accounts of their travels and described the city, the palace and the garden. But all of them wrote most highly of the nightingale. "That is the best of all," they said.

One day, one of these books was sent to the Emperor as a gift.

11

He sat in his golden chair and read and read, nodding his head wisely, for he liked to read of his city, his palace and his garden. "But the nightingale is best of all," he read at the end.

"What's this?" exclaimed the Emperor. "I don't know the nightingale. What is this bird in my garden? To think that I should first learn about it from a book!"

He called his chief chamberlain. "They say there is a wonderful bird in my garden. They say it is the best thing in my whole empire. Why have I never been told about it?"

"I do not know the bird," said the chamberlain.

"I command that he shall sing before me at court this evening," said the Emperor.

"Certainly," said the chamberlain. "He shall be brought."

But where was he? The chamberlain ran up stairs and along corridors. He asked everybody he met where he would find the nightingale, but nobody could tell him. At length he returned to the Emperor. "Nobody has heard of the nightingale, Your Highness," he said. "The writer of the book must have invented him."

"Nonsense," said the Emperor. "The book was presented to me by his Imperial Majesty, the Emperor of Japan. It cannot be an invention. I insist that the nightingale is brought before me this evening, otherwise all the court shall be trampled on after supper."

Again the chamberlain ran up and down the staircases, through halls and receiving rooms, and half the court ran with him, for they did not want to be trampled on. At last they came to the kitchens where they met a little kitchen-maid.

"The nightingale?" she said. "I know it well. Every evening I visit my mother with scraps of food, and when I am walking back to the palace I often rest in the woods. Then I hear the nightingale sing. And tears come into my eyes for I feel just as if my mother had kissed me."

"Little kitchen-maid," said the chamberlain, "I will get you a better position in the kitchen if you will lead me to the nightingale for the Emperor expects him this evening."

So they all followed the little kitchen-maid to the woods. On the way a cow began to moo. "There it is!" cried the pages. "It's amazing to think that such a small creature should have such a powerful voice!"

"No," said the little kitchen-maid. "That is a cow. We are a long way from the place yet."

Now some frogs began to croak in the marsh. "Listen!" they all said. "It sounds like church bells."

"No. Those are frogs," said the little kitchen-maid.

And then the nightingale began to sing.

"There it is!" exclaimed the little girl. "Listen! Listen! Look, there it is, up there!" And she pointed to the little reddish-brown bird up in the boughs.

"Is it possible," said the chamberlain, "that such an ordinary little bird should sing like that?"

"Little nightingale," said the little kitchen-maid, "our gracious Emperor wants you to sing to him."

"With pleasure," replied the nightingale. And it began to sing most beautifully.

"It sounds like glass bells," said the chamberlain. "I cannot believe we have never heard it before."

"Shall I sing again for the Emperor?" asked the nightingale, for it thought the Emperor was listening.

"My little nightingale," said the chamberlain. "It is my privilege to invite you to a court festival this evening when you shall sing before his Imperial Majesty."

"My song sounds best in the woods," replied the nightingale. But it agreed to come to the court.

That evening everyone was gathered in the great hall. Even the little kitchen-maid was allowed to stand behind a door. A golden perch had been placed in front of the Emperor's golden chair, and on this the nightingale sat. The Emperor nodded to the nightingale.

And the nightingale sang so wonderfully that the Emperor's

eyes filled with tears. Then the nightingale sang even more
sweetly and the music went straight to the Emperor's heart. The
Emperor was so pleased that he said the nightingale could wear
his golden slipper round its neck.

But the nightingale said that seeing the Emperor's eyes fill with
tears was a sufficient reward.

The Emperor decided that the nightingale should stay at court.
It would have its own golden cage and would be allowed to go out
twice a day and once at night. When the nightingale went out,
twelve servants each held tightly to silken threads tied to
the bird's leg. It was no fun for the nightingale to go out like
that.

One day, the Emperor received a large parcel, labelled simply,
"NIGHTINGALE."

When the parcel was opened they found a box and inside the
box was a jewelled nightingale, brilliantly decorated with diamonds and rubies and sapphires. When the bird was wound up it
sang beautiful melodies, and its tail moved up and down in time to
the music.

"How wonderful!" everyone said. "They must sing a duet."

And so they did. But it did not sound very well, for the real nightingale sang as he had always sung, from the heart, and the jewelled bird sang waltzes.

Now the jewelled bird was to sing alone. It was just as successful as the real nightingale and much handsomer to look at, for it gleamed like a necklace. It sang the same piece thirty-three times and was not tired.

Then the Emperor said it was the living nightingale's turn. But where was it? Nobody had noticed it fly away through the open window, back to the wood.

"What an ungrateful creature!" exclaimed the courtiers. "But we have the best bird, anyhow," they all agreed. And they listened to it again. For the jewelled bird always sang the same tunes, so they knew what was coming, but with a real nightingale you never know what it will sing next.

The following Sunday the Emperor agreed that the jewelled bird should be shown to the people. The bird was wound up and sang to them and they were pleased. But the poor fisherman said to himself, "It sounds all right, but the tunes are all the same. Something is missing."

The real nightingale was banished from the country and the artificial bird was set on a velvet cushion beside the Emperor's bed, and was given the title of "Lord High After Dinner Singer".

A whole year passed. Every person in the palace and the city knew every little twitter in the jewelled bird's song by heart. Little boys sang "Tsi-tsi-tsi-glug-glug!" in the streets, and the Emperor sang it himself too.

Then, one evening when the Emperor was lying in bed listening to the jewelled bird singing, something inside the bird went, "Twang!" All the little wheels whirred round, there was a click and the singing stopped.

The Emperor leapt out of bed. He called the court doctor, but what could *he* do? A watchmaker was sent for. He opened up the artificial bird, put in new wheels and cogs and springs, and the bird sang a little, but not so sweetly as before. The watchmaker said it must be treated very carefully for the barrels were nearly worn out and it would be impossible to put in new ones. The bird must be allowed to sing only once a year. Everybody agreed that once a year was better than never.

Five years passed and a new sorrow came to the people: the Emperor was very ill and could not, it was said, live very much longer. A new Emperor was chosen and people were treating him as if the old Emperor were already dead.

But he was not dead. He lay, stiff and pale, on his great bed with the long velvet curtains. The jewelled bird sat beside him on its velvet cushion and high up through an open window the moon shone down.

The Emperor could hardly breathe. He felt as if something heavy was lying on his chest. He opened his eyes and saw that it was Death that was sitting there. And all around him were his good and bad deeds, waiting.

"Music!" cried the Emperor. "Music! My precious jewelled bird, sing to me." But the bird stayed silent for no one was there to wind it up. And Death continued to stare at the Emperor with his hollow eyes.

Suddenly, from the window there came a sound. A song. A beautiful song. It was the little live nightingale sitting on a branch. It had heard of the Emperor's illness and had come to sing to him, to bring him hope. As it sang, warmth began to come back to the Emperor's cheeks, his legs felt stronger; even Death listened.

The nightingale sang on and on. It sang of a garden where white roses grow, where the flowers smell sweet, where the grass is watered by tears. Then Death felt a longing to see his garden and floated out of the window in a white mist.

"Thank you, little nightingale," said the Emperor. "I banished you from my country, but you have banished Death from my heart. How can I reward you?"

"When I first sang to you, I brought tears to your eyes," said the nightingale. "That is sufficient reward. Sleep now, and grow strong, and I will sing to you again."

And it sang, and the Emperor slept. The sun rose and shone through the window and when the Emperor awoke he felt refreshed and strong. Not one servant came, for they all thought he was dead. Only the little nightingale sat beside him and sang.

"Stay with me," said the Emperor. "I will break the artificial bird into a thousand pieces."

"No," said the nightingale. "I cannot live in a palace. Keep your jewelled bird, and let me come whenever I wish, to sing to you. I will sing of happiness and sorrow, of good and evil. I want to be able to sing to you and to the poor fisherman and the humble peasant. You must promise me only one thing."

"Anything!" said the Emperor. He stood at the window in his robes, for he had dressed himself.

"One thing only," said the nightingale. "Do not tell anyone that you have a little bird who tells you everything." Then the nightingale flew away.

The door opened and the servants came in to look at their dead Emperor.

"Good morning," he said.

THE FIR TREE

Out in the forest stood a pretty little fir tree. It was surrounded by other trees, larger and grander, pines as well as firs. The fir tree was not happy. It longed to be taller. It did not care for the warm sunshine and the fresh air. It did not enjoy the little children who came out to the woods looking for wild strawberries and raspberries. Sometimes they found a whole cupful, then they would sit down beside the little fir tree and say, "How pretty and small thisone is." The little fir tree did not like to hear that at all.

Next year it had grown taller, and the following year it was taller still.

"Oh if only I were a great tall tree like the others," sighed the little fir tree. "Then I could spread my branches out wide, and birds would build their nests in my boughs."

When it was winter and snow lay all around, a hare would come jumping and spring right over the little fir tree. This made the tree so angry. But in a few years the hare had to run round the little tree.

In the autumn, woodcutters came and felled the largest trees. Their branches were cut off and they were laid on wagons and dragged away. Where were they going? When the swallows and stork came in the spring, the tree asked them: "Do you know where the trees were taken?" And the stork said, "As I·was flying over the sea I met many ships with stately masts that smelt like fir. I fancy these were the trees."

"Oh, if only I were big enough to go over the sea! What is the sea? What does it look like?"

"It would take too long to explain," said the stork. And he flew away.

When Christmastime came several quite young trees were felled. These trees kept all their branches; they were put on wagons and horses dragged them out of the wood. "Where are they going?" asked the fir tree. "Some of them are no bigger than I am. Why have they kept their branches?"

"We know that," chirped the sparrows. "They are taken to the town and dressed up in great finery. They are planted in a warm room and decorated with golden apples, honey cakes, little toys and hundreds of candles."

"And after that?" asked the little tree. "What happens after that?"

"We don't know. We haven't seen any more."

"Oh!" cried the little fir tree. "Oh, if only I could be planted in a warm room and be decorated with hundreds of candles."

"Be happy where you are," said the air and sunshine. "Enjoy your youth here in the woodland."

But the fir tree did not rejoice at all.

It grew and grew and people who saw it said: "That's a handsome tree." And when Christmastime came round again the little fir tree was cut down first of all. It fell to the ground with a sigh and felt quite faint. It could not dream of happiness for it was now so sad to be parting from all its friends in the woodland.

When it came to, it was being unloaded in a yard and two servants carried it into a large beautiful room. Pictures hung all

round the walls and the floor was covered with a richly patterned carpet. The fir tree was put in a tub filled with sand, and the tub was wrapped in a green cloth. Then the tree was decorated. More than a hundred little candles were fastened to the boughs. Nets filled with sweets, apples and nuts hung down from the branches. Dolls swung among the green pine needles and at the very tip-top of the tree was fastened a golden star.

"Tonight everything will gleam with light," they said.

"Oh," thought the tree. "When will night come? Will the sparrows come and look at me through the windows? Will I stay here for ever in this beautiful room?"

At last the candles were lighted. What brilliance! The tree trembled so much that one of the candles set a green twig alight. But the fire was soon put out.

Then the big doors were opened and a number of children rushed in. They danced round the tree, shouting and laughing. As the candles burned down they were snuffed out and at last the children were given permission to strip the tree. They rushed upon it, seizing the fruits and pretty toys until only the star at the top remained. The children danced about and no one looked at the tree except one old servant, who only looked to see if by chance an apple or a bag of nuts had been forgotten.

"A story, a story!" shouted the children, pulling a smiling little man towards the tree. He sat down just beneath it. "The tree can listen to the story too," he said. "Now, do you want the story of the Goose who laid Golden Eggs or of Klumpey Dumpey who fell downstairs and married a princess?" "The Goose," cried some, and "Klumpey Dumpey!" cried others. "Klumpey Dumpey, it shall be," said the little man. The fir tree stood silently and listened to the story of Klumpey Dumpey who married a princess. And it

looked forward to the following evening when it would be dressed again with candles and toys and fruit. Perhaps it would hear another story. All night the tree stood silent and thoughtful.

In the morning two servants came in and dragged the tree out of the room and upstairs to the attic where it was flung in a dark corner. "What is the meaning of this?" thought the tree. "What am I going to do here?" And it leaned against a wall and thought and thought.

"It is winter now. The earth is hard and covered with snow and people cannot plant me until the spring. I suppose I am to be left until then. My little hare will be jumping in the wood now. If only I were not so lonely here."

"Piep! Piep!" said two little mice. They smelt the tree and crept among the branches. "Who are you?" they said. "And where have you come from? Tell us about the most beautiful place on earth. Have you been there?" And the tree told the little mice all about life in the forest.

"Oh! How happy you must have been!" they said. "Yes," said the fir tree. "Yes. I was happy." Then it told of Christmas Eve when it had been hung with sweets and fruit and candles.

"What splendid stories you can tell," they said and the next night they came back with four more little mice and the fir tree told its story all over again. Then it told them the story of Klumpey Dumpey who fell downstairs and married a princess. The little mice were ready to jump to the top of the tree with delight. The next night a great many more mice came and on Sunday even two rats appeared. But they didn't enjoy the story so much, and the mice did not like it so much as before.

"Do you only know one story?" asked the rats.

"Only one," said the tree. "I heard it on the happiest evening of my life."

"It's not a very good story," they said. "Don't you know any stories about bacon and cheese?"

"No," said the tree.

So they went away and the tree was left alone.

One morning, people came and rummaged in the attic. They dragged the tree down the stairs to a courtyard where the sun was shining. The courtyard was next to a garden where flowers were blooming and birds were singing. "Now I shall live again," thought the tree. And it tried to spread its branches, but they were yellow and brittle. It lay in a corner among the nettles. Two boys ran up and one tore off the star that still clung to the topmost branch.

The tree looked at the flowers and it looked at itself and wished it had stayed in the dark attic. And then it remembered its youth in the wood. "All past. If only I had rejoiced when I could have done."

Then a servant came and chopped the tree into little pieces and the whole bundle was placed under the stove where it blazed brightly. As it burned, it sighed and each sigh was a little "puff! puff!" as the tree thought of summer days and winter nights, and of Christmas Eve and Klumpey Dumpey, the only story it had ever heard or told.

The boys played in the garden and on his breast the little one had a golden star which the tree had worn on its happiest evening.

THE CONSTANT TIN SOLDIER

Once upon a time there was a box with twenty-five soldiers lying shoulder to shoulder inside. They were brothers for they had all been born out of one old tin spoon. Their uniforms were red and blue and they shouldered their muskets and looked straight

ahead: they were very grand. The first words they heard in the world were, "Tin soldiers!" These were shouted by a little boy when he took the lid off the box one day. It was his birthday. He took each soldier out of the box and placed it on the table. Every one was exactly like his brothers, except the last. There had not been quite enough tin to finish him, but he stood just as proudly on his one leg as his brothers on their two. And it is this soldier who has the adventures.

When the little boy put the soldiers on the table the first thing they saw was a fine castle. You could peep through the little windows into a hall, and round the walls were four towers with battlements. In front of the castle lay a mirror which was the lake. Around the lake some little green trees had been placed and on the lake were swimming swans made of wax.

At the entrance to the castle there was a little paper lady. She was wearing a dress of fine net with a tiny blue ribbon round her shoulders. In the middle of the ribbon was a shining tinsel rose. The little lady raised both her arms, for she was a dancer. Then she lifted one leg so high that the tin soldier could not see it at all, and he thought that, like himself, she had only one leg.

"That's the wife for me," he thought. "But she lives in a castle, and I have only a box, and besides there are twenty-five of us already. There's no room for her as well."

The soldier lay down at full length behind a snuff box that was also on the table. From there he could easily watch the little lady who continued to stand quite steadily on her one leg.

When bedtime came all the other soldiers were put away in the box, but the tin soldier still lay behind the snuff box, never taking his eyes off the little lady who stood up straight on the point of one of her toes. Now the toys began to play at "going visiting": the dolls chattered, the pencil amused itself on the drawing board, and there was so much noise that even the canary woke up. The only two who did not move were the tin soldier and the dancing lady.

Just then, the clock struck twelve! Pop! Off came the lid of the snuff box and out bounced a little goblin.

"Tin soldier," he said. "Stop staring at things that are no business of yours."

But the tin soldier pretended not to hear him.

"Just you wait till tomorrow!" said the goblin.

In the morning, when the children got up, the tin soldier was placed on the windowsill. Suddenly the window flew open and the soldier fell headlong from the third floor to the street below. Whether it was the goblin or the wind that did it, who can tell? The soldier was stuck with his one leg in the air and his helmet and his bayonet wedged between a crack in the paving stones.

The little boy ran down the stairs to look for him, but even though he nearly trod on him he did not see him.

Then it started to rain. Great big drops fell and soon the streets and pavements were running with water. But at last it stopped and two boys passing by spotted the soldier, wedged as he was.

"Look at that!" they said. "Let's make him a boat."

They made a boat out of newspaper, stood the tin soldier in it and sailed it down the gutter. The boys ran alongside as the boat rocked up and down in the water. Sometimes it turned round and round and the tin soldier trembled, but he stood firm, looked straight ahead and shouldered his musket as proudly as ever.

Then the boat went into a drain under the road, and it was as dark as if the soldier had been in his box. "Oh, if only the little lady were with me now," he thought. "What would the darkness matter then?"

Suddenly, in front of him was a large, fat water rat that lived under the drain.

"Show your passport," said the rat. "Where's your passport?"

The tin soldier said nothing, but he held his musket more tightly than ever.

The boat was now going faster and the tin soldier could see daylight at the end of the drain. Then he heard a roaring noise, where the drain poured into a deep canal. But his paper boat was so close it could not stop and in a moment the tin soldier was engulfed in water. The little paper boat sank deeper and deeper and began to break up. The soldier closed his eyes and thought of the pretty little dancer. He would never see her again. At last the boat fell apart and the tin soldier fell out and was immediately snapped up by a large fish.

Now it was darker than ever, much darker than in the drain

tunnel. The tin soldier lay stiffly in the fish's body.

The fish swam to and fro and then suddenly became quite still. After a time something flashed through the fish and daylight shone again. The tin soldier heard a voice exclaim, "Look at this! It's the tin soldier!" For the fish had been caught, taken to market, bought, taken into the kitchen where it had been cut open with a sharp knife. The cook lifted out the soldier, rinsed him in water and carried him upstairs. Then she placed him on the table in the very room where he had been before. He saw the same children, his brother soldiers, the castle with the little dancer, still balancing on the toes of her one leg. He looked at her, but they did not speak.

One of the little boys suddenly picked up the soldier and flung him into the stove. Why did he do this? No one knows. It must have been the goblin's fault.

The soldier stood there among the hot coals. Through the door of the stove he could see the little dancer. He looked at her and she looked at him. He could feel himself melting, though whether it was from love or the heat of the stove he was not sure, but still he shouldered his musket and stood firm. Suddenly a gust of air caught the little lady and she was blown straight into the stove beside the tin soldier. In a spurt of flame she was gone. And the tin soldier melted into a solid lump. The next morning when the maid cleaned out the ashes she found the lump in the shape of a little tin heart. But nothing remained of the little dancer except the tinsel rose, and that was black as black.

THUMBELINA

✤

Once there was a woman who longed for a child, but it did not look as if she would have one. So she went to an old witch and said, "I do so want a little child. Can you tell me how I may get one?"

"Oh, that's no problem," said the witch. "Take this stem of barley. Pop it into a flowerpot and watch what happens."

"Thank you," said the woman; and she went home and planted the barley in a flowerpot. Immediately a strong shoot sprang up that looked as if it were a tulip but the leaves were tightly closed.

"That's very interesting," said the woman and she kissed the red and green leaves. As she kissed them the leaves sprang open revealing a beautiful red tulip, and in the middle of the flower sat a delicate and tiny young girl, so small she was scarcely the length of your thumb. The woman called her Thumbelina.

At night Thumbelina slept in a polished walnut shell; the mattress was made of violet leaves and the coverlet was rose petals. During the day she played on the table where the woman had arranged a dish with flowers around the edge. The dish was filled with water where the flowers' stalks stood. On the water was a tulip leaf and on this Thumbelina liked to sit, rowing herself across with two white horse hairs for oars.

One night, as Thumbelina lay in her walnut-shell bed, an old

toad came creeping through the window. The toad was big, ugly and damp. It climbed on to the table where Thumbelina lay.

"She would make a very fine wife for my son," thought the toad and she took the walnut shell, and Thumbelina, away with her through the window.

At the bottom of the garden was a wide brook, where many water lilies grew. The banks were muddy and soft and marsh marigolds and bog irises flourished. Here the toad lived with her son. When the son saw Thumbelina lying in the walnut shell, he started to croak with joy. "Brek-kek-ke-kex," he said over and over again. "Brek-kek-ke-kex."

"Don't make so much noise," said his mother, "or she will wake up, and she might run away. Let's put her on one of the lily-leaves in the brook. Then she will be stranded on an island and won't be able to get away. In the meantime we can start preparing the bridal suite for your wedding night."

In the middle of the brook grew the largest leaves and to one of these the toad swam with Thumbelina, still in her walnut shell. When Thumbelina awoke in the morning and saw where she was, she began to cry, for she was completely surrounded by water and she could not possibly get to land. Meanwhile the old toad and her son were busily preparing the best room, which was to be made very pretty for the bride. Then the toad swam out to the lily-leaf with her son who bowed to Thumbelina. "Croak-croak-croak," he said. The old toad took Thumbelina's walnut shell bed so that it would be ready for her when she came to live in the marsh with her son. And Thumbelina sat all alone on the lily-leaf and wept.

But under the lily-leaves were shoals of little fishes. They had heard what the old toad had said and felt very sorry for Thumbelina who was to be forced to marry the toad's ugly son. They put their heads out of the water to look at the girl who was to be the toad's bride and when they saw how pretty she was they all agreed that the wedding must not happen.

They surrounded the green stalk of the lily-leaf on which Thumbelina was sitting and together they gnawed away at the stalk until at last the leaf sailed away downstream, and away went Thumbelina too, where the toad could not get at her.

She floated on in the sunshine, past meadows and towns, watching the shadows dancing on the water. Then suddenly a big May bug came flying past. He saw Thumbelina, wrapped his arms around her waist and flew with her up into a tree. The green leaf continued down the stream on its own.

You can imagine how frightened Thumbelina was. The May bug seated her upon the largest leaf in the tree, found honey in the flowers for her and told her how pretty she was. Then all the other May bugs in the tree came to visit. When they saw Thumbelina they said: "Why! She has only four legs! And where are her feelers? And her wings?"

"She looks almost like a human! How ugly she is!" said the lady May bugs.

Even the May bug who had carried her off began to believe them, though deep down he knew Thumbelina was very pretty. So they flew down with her from the tree and sat her on a daisy, where they left her. And Thumbelina wept because the May bugs had said she was so ugly.

All through the summer Thumbelina was quite alone in the wood. She wove a bed for herself out of blades of grass which she hung up between two stalks of cow parsley. She drank the dew in the morning and ate the honey from the flowers. But at last the summer gave way to autumn and soon it was winter, the long, cold winter. The birds had flown away, the flowers had died, and the tall cow parsley on which she had hung her hammock bed was nothing but a yellow stalk. Her clothes were torn and even though she wrapped herself in a dry withered leaf she was dreadfully cold.

Close to the wood was a large cornfield. The corn had been cut long ago and only the sharp stubble remained. This was like a forest for Thumbelina to go through. But suddenly she came to the door of a field mouse's home which was snug and comfortable under the stubble. There was a warm kitchen and a larder full of provisions for the long winter. Thumbelina stood at the door and begged for a small morsel of corn, for she had not eaten for two days.

"You poor little creature," said the field mouse. "You had better come in and warm yourself." The field mouse soon decided she liked Thumbelina and she said, "If you like, you may stay with me all through the winter, but you must keep the kitchen clean and tidy, and you must tell me stories in the evenings."

Thumbelina agreed and was very happy with the kind old field mouse.

"Soon we shall have a visitor," said the field mouse one day. "My friend comes quite regularly to see me. He is far richer than I, and has a large house with a great many rooms, and he has beautiful black velvet fur. If you could persuade him to marry you, you would be very well off. You must tell him the best stories you know."

But Thumbelina was not happy about this. She did not care for the friend, who was a mole. The field mouse was always telling her how rich he was, how learned, how clever, but he did not like sunshine and beautiful flowers for he had never seen them. The mole asked Thumbelina to sing and she sang, "Ladybird, ladybird, fly away home," and the mole fell in love with her because of her beautiful voice. But he said nothing.

Sometime before this, he had dug a passage from his house to theirs and Thumbelina and the field mouse were invited to walk in it whenever they wished. In the passage lay a swallow, dead from the cold, with his lovely blue wings pressed to the sides of his body, and his head and feet drawn back under his feathers. The mole pushed his nose up through the roof so that a shaft of daylight shone down. Thumbelina looked at the swallow sadly, but the mole gave him a push and said, "That's the end of him and his twittering. How awful to be born a bird, only to cheep all through the summer and in the winter to die of cold."

"Yes, indeed," agreed the field mouse. "What's the use of 'cheep-cheep-cheep' when the ground is hard with frost?"

Thumbelina said nothing. But when the other two had continued on down the passage she knelt beside the swallow, pushed his feathers aside and kissed his closed eyelids. "Perhaps you are one of the birds who sang to me in the summer," she whispered.

The mole then closed up the hole he had made in the roof and they went home. That night when she was in bed, Thumbelina could not sleep for thinking of the swallow. She got up and prepared a covering of hay which she quietly spread over the dead bird. "Goodbye, you beautiful creature," she said. "Thank you for your songs in the summer when the sun shone, the trees were green and the flowers bloomed." And she lay down beside the swallow with her head on his breast.

But the swallow was not dead, only stiff with cold. In the autumn, swallows fly south to warmer countries where they spend the winter. But if one stays too long, the cold attacks it and it falls to the ground, and eventually dies.

As Thumbelina lay there, the swallow stirred. Thumbelina trembled with fear, for the swallow was huge compared to her, who was only the height of your thumb. But she was brave, tucked the hay more closely round the bird and brought a leaf, the coverlet from her own bed, and laid it on the swallow's head.

The following night she crept to see him again. The swallow was definitely alive, but very weak and he could only keep his eyes open for a moment. "Thank you, my child," he said. "Thank you for bringing me warmth. Soon I shall get my strength back and then I shall be able to fly about once more."

"Oh, no," said Thumbelina. "It is far too cold to fly about. There is snow on the ground and everywhere is frozen hard. You stay here and I will look after you."

She brought the swallow water in a flower petal and he told her how he had hurt one of his wings in a thorn tree and had not been able to fly as fast as the others. At last he had fallen to the ground and remembered nothing until Thumbelina revived him.

The swallow stayed there the whole winter and neither the field mouse nor the mole knew that the swallow was alive, for they weren't interested. When the spring came and the earth was warmer, Thumbelina opened up the hole the mole had made in the roof. The sun shone in on them and the swallow asked Thumbelina if she would come with him and they could fly away together. But Thumbelina knew that she could not leave the old field mouse.

"Goodbye," said the swallow, and he flew out through the hole into the sunshine. Thumbelina watched him as he flew out of sight and tears came into her eyes. She felt very sad. She was not allowed to go out into the sunshine. Corn had been sown in the field over the field mouse's house and it would have been quite impossible for Thumbelina to struggle through the stalks.

"My friend the mole wants to marry you," said the field mouse one day. "How lucky you are! Now you must start preparing for your wedding. You must have plenty of new clothes, for if you are to be the mole's wife you must always look your best."

Four spiders were hired to weave for Thumbelina day and night. Every evening the mole paid her a visit, and every evening he said that when the weather was a little cooler and the sun not quite so hot, they would get married. But Thumbelina was sad for she did not want to marry the boring old mole one little bit. Every morning and evening she crept out of the door and when the wind blew the corn stalks apart and she could see the blue sky she thought how beautiful it was out there. If only she could see her swallow again. But the swallow did not appear – he was probably far away somewhere high up above the trees.

When autumn came Thumbelina had her wedding outfit ready. "Your wedding is in four weeks," said the field mouse.

But Thumbelina wept and said she would not be the wife of the mole. "Nonsense," said the field mouse. "He is a fine, handsome man. Nobody has such beautiful velvet fur. His cellar and store-rooms are full. You are a very lucky girl."

At last the day arrived. The mole came to fetch Thumbelina. Never again would she see the warm sunshine, for the mole only liked to live deep underground. For the last time she went to the field mouse's doorway and stretched her arms to the sun. She walked out into the cornfield, which had now been cut and where only the stubble remained. "Farewell, bright sun," she said. "Farewell," and she put her arms around a scarlet poppy which was still flowering. "Greet the swallow for me if you see him again."

"Tweet! Tweet! Tweet! Tweet!" said a voice overhead. Thumbelina looked up and there was the swallow! She told him how she was to marry the ugly mole who lived deep under the earth where the sun never shone. She could not stop herself from crying; she was so unhappy.

"The cold weather is coming," said the swallow. "I am going to fly to warmer countries. Why don't you come with me? You can sit on my back and we can fly away from the mole and his dark house, far away over the mountains, to warm lands, where the sun is hot and where there are beautiful flowers. Do come with me, Thumbelina."

"Yes, I will come with you," she said, and she climbed on the bird's back, put her feet on his wing and tied her belt tightly to one of his feathers. And the swallow flew high in the air, over the forests and the sea, over the mountains where the snow never melts, and Thumbelina hid among the swallow's feathers, only putting her head out to peep at the land below.

At last they came to warm countries. There the sun seemed far brighter, the sky was bluer and rich fruits grew on the trees. The air was full of the scent of herbs. But the swallow flew on further until they came to a lake beside which stood a white marble palace. Vines twined around the pillars and at the top of one of the pillars was the nest of the swallow who carried Thumbelina.

"This is my house," he said, "but you cannot live here. I must make it tidy and neat. Choose one of the flowers down there and I will put you into it." Below them a marble pillar had fallen to the ground and among the broken pieces huge white flowers grew. The swallow flew down with Thumbelina and put her on one of the broad green leaves.

To Thumbelina's amazement, in the midst of the flower sat a tiny man. On his head was a golden crown and from his shoulders

grew bright wings, like a butterfly's. He was the king of all the flowers, in each of which lived a tiny man or woman.

''How handsome he is!'' whispered Thumbelina to the swallow. When the little man saw Thumbelina he was enchanted. Never before had he seen such a beautiful girl. He took off his crown, placed it on Thumbelina's head and asked her if she would be his wife. She agreed immediately, for this would be a very different husband from the old toad's son or the mole with black velvet fur.

Straightaway, out of each flower came a lord or lady and each one brought a present for Thumbelina; but the best present was a pair of white wings which were fastened to her shoulders, and now she too could flutter from flower to flower.

Everybody rejoiced at the marriage, and above them in his nest sat the swallow singing his wedding song. Later, when the swallow flew away again, far away back to Denmark, he returned to his nest over the window of the man who tells fairy tales, and told him the whole story of Thumbelina.

THE EMPEROR'S NEW CLOTHES

Many years ago there lived an emperor who thought of nothing but clothes. He spent all his money on them. He had a different coat for each hour of the day. Whereas other emperors would be busy with affairs of state, this one was always at his tailor's.

The town where he lived was very lively, and many visitors came to go to the theatre or to admire the handsome buildings. One day two scoundrels arrived. They said they were weavers who could weave the finest cloth imaginable. Not only were the patterns and designs incredibly beautiful, but any clothes made

from the cloth possessed the magical quality that they were invisible to any person who was stupid or unfit for his job.

"These must be very wonderful clothes," thought the Emperor. "If I had a suit of such clothes I should be able to find out which of my ministers were not fit for their job." And he asked the two scoundrels to weave cloth for a new suit of clothes without delay. He gave them a great deal of money to buy the finest silks and the most expensive trimmings. This the scoundrels put in their bags.

Then they set up two looms and pretended to be very hard at work. In fact they did nothing at all! The Emperor longed to know how they were getting on but was nervous of going to see for himself. "It would be better," he thought, "to send someone else first." So he sent his most trusted minister. "He has very good sense," thought the Emperor. "Nobody is better qualified than he to judge the quality of the work."

So the good old minister went into the room where the two scoundrels were pretending to work. He opened his eyes wide, for of course he could see nothing at all. The scoundrels invited him to admire the cloth, the exquisite pattern, the beautiful design. "Oh, yes, very fine, quite enchanting," said the minister, but inside he was thinking, "Am I unfit for my job? Am I stupid? No, I cannot admit that I can see nothing." He peered through his spectacles and praised the cloth.

"I shall tell the Emperor how beautiful it is and how pleased he will be with it."

And this he did.

Then the scoundrels asked for more money and more silks, but they kept it all for themselves, and continued to work at the empty

looms. The Emperor sent another faithful servant to inspect the work. And of course he too could see nothing.

"Is it not a beautiful piece of cloth?" said the two scoundrels. And the servant agreed that it was enchanting. "This is ludicrous," he thought. "I must not let anyone know that I am unfit for my job." And he returned to the Emperor, full of praise for the lovely cloth.

Soon the whole town was talking about the magic cloth and the Emperor decided that he must see it for himself. With a great following of faithful servants, including the minister and the servant who had already been there, he went to the room where the two cunning scoundrels were weaving away with might and main, without any threads.

"Isn't it beautiful?" said the old minister. "Is not Your Majesty delighted with the pattern and the rich tones?" And he pointed at

the empty loom, for he thought that everybody else could see the stuff.

"What's this?" thought the Emperor. "I can see nothing. This is terrible. Am I stupid? Am I unfit to be Emperor?"

"Oh, it is lovely," he said aloud. "It will look very fine when made up into a suit." And he nodded and gazed at the empty loom, for he could not say that he could see nothing at all. Everybody admired the wonderful cloth and persuaded the Emperor to wear the new clothes in the grand procession that was to take place in a few days' time. There was general rejoicing and the Emperor gave the two scoundrels the title of Weavers to the Imperial Court.

On the night before the procession, the scoundrels were hard at work all night long. They had sixteen candles burning and everybody could see how busy they were, completing the Emperor's new clothes. They pretended to take the cloth off the looms; they snipped the air with great scissors; they sewed using needles without thread; and at last they said: "The Emperor's new clothes are ready."

The Emperor and his faithful courtiers went in, and the two scoundrels held up their arms as if they were showing off the clothes. "See, here are the trousers, and the coat. This is the cloak; look how light it is. They are all as light as cobwebs. One almost feels as if one has nothing on."

"Yes, indeed," said all the courtiers.

"Would Your Majesty like to try the clothes on now?" the scoundrels asked. "Then you could see yourself in the great mirror and we can check the fit of the garments."

The Emperor took off the clothes he was wearing and the two scoundrels pretended to dress him in his new clothes. "Oh, how handsome you look! What elegance! What style!'' everyone exclaimed. And the Emperor admired himself once more in the mirror.

Then the Emperor went outside to join the procession. Two lords pretended to pick up the train of the Emperor's cloak and hold it in their hands, and the Emperor marched in the procession under a beautiful canopy. All the townspeople exclaimed as he passed, ''What a wonderful long train! How splendid the Emperor's new clothes are! How well they fit him!'' No one would let his friends think that he was a fool or unfit for his job. No Emperor's new clothes were ever admired as much as these were.

''But he has nothing on at all,'' said a little boy. The crowd nearby heard him and whispered to each other: ''A little boy says the Emperor has nothing on at all!'' Soon everybody was whispering: ''The Emperor has nothing on!''

The Emperor heard the people whispering and he knew they were right. But he held his head high and walked on. And the two lords held up the train that was not there at all.

THE WILD SWANS

Far away in a land over the sea there lived a king who had eleven sons and one daughter, the Princess Eliza. The eleven brothers were princes and went to school wearing a star on their tunics and carrying a sword by their sides. They wrote with diamond pencils on their slates, while their sister Eliza sat on a shining glass stool reading from a picture book which had cost half a kingdom. The children were very happy and much loved.

But their father, the king, married a bad queen who did not love the children at all. They knew this immediately for even at the wedding feast the queen gave orders that they were to be given only sand in a teacup and were told to pretend that it was something nice.

The following week the queen took little Eliza out into the country and left her with a poor peasant and his wife; and in a very short while she had told the king so many wicked lies about the young princes that he did not bother with them anymore.

"Fly out into the wide world

and find your own food," said the queen. "Fly like great birds and be gone."

With a strange cry they became eleven beautiful wild swans and flew out of the palace, over the woods and away.

Early in the morning they came to the cottage where their sister Eliza was asleep in the little room under the roof. They stretched their long necks and flapped their wings, but no one heard or saw them, and they flew on, high up among the clouds until they came to the sea.

Eliza stayed in the cottage with the poor peasants until she was fifteen years old. She had nothing to do, nothing to play with and nothing to read, but as the years passed she grew more and more beautiful. Eventually she went home to the palace. When the queen saw how beautiful she was, she was filled with hatred towards her and would have liked to change her into a swan too, but she didn't dare, because she knew the king wanted to see his daughter.

So the queen went to the bathroom, which was made of white marble. She took three toads, kissed them and spoke to them one by one. To the first she said, "When Eliza comes to take her bath, sit upon her hair that she may be as stupid as you are." To the second she said, "Sit on her forehead that she may be as ugly as you are and her father will not recognize her." And to the third she said, "Sit on her heart that she may have an evil mind."

She put the toads into the water which at once turned green. When Eliza stepped into the water and lay down, one of the toads sat upon her hair, another upon her forehead, and the third on her heart, but she didn't seem to notice. And when she stepped out of the water, three poppies were floating on it. Eliza was so sweet and good that the queen's sorcery did not work and the three toads had turned into flowers.

When the queen saw that her spell had failed, she rubbed Eliza's skin with walnut juice so that it became dark brown and she tangled her hair so that it hung in a matted confusion. It was impossible to recognize her. And when her father saw her he turned away and said that she could not possibly be his daughter. Only the old dog knew her, and nobody listened to him!

Eliza wept and thought of her eleven brothers who had been driven away. She walked slowly and sadly out of the palace and across the moors to the great wood. She longed for her brothers and decided to set out to look for them.

Eliza had been in the wood only a little while when night fell. She lay down on soft moss, leaned her head against a tree stump and fell asleep. Glow-worms shone above her like twinkling stars. All night long she dreamed of her brothers: they were children again, writing with their diamond pencils and reading from the beautiful picture book which had cost half a kingdom. But in the dream everything on the page came alive and acted out all that had happened to Eliza and her brothers.

When Eliza awoke the sun was high in the sky, although the leaves overhead protected her from the direct sunlight. The sunshine played upon the ground and birds sang just above her head. She could hear water rippling: the sound came from several springs all running down to a lake surrounded by bushes, through which the deer had made a hole when they went to the lake to drink. Here Eliza went down to the water. The lake was crystal clear and every leaf and branch was mirrored in its shining surface. When Eliza saw her own face reflected there, she was horrified. But she dipped her hands in the water and rubbed her eyes and her forehead and soon her own skin shone through the

dye. She took off her clothes and stepped into the sparkling water.

When she had dressed herself again and plaited her long hair, she drank from one of the springs out of her cupped hands. Then she wandered deep into the woods, not knowing where she was going. She thought of her brothers and prayed that she would one day see them again. She found a wild apple tree whose boughs reached down to the ground with the weight of the fruit. Then she went on deeper into the wood where the trees were so close together the sunlight could scarcely pierce them. When darkness fell, it was a thick, black dark. No glow-worms could be seen. Sadly she lay down to rest.

In the morning she had taken only a few steps when she met an old woman with berries in her basket. Eliza asked her if she had seen eleven princes riding through the woods.

"No," replied the old woman, "but yesterday I saw eleven swans swimming in the river nearby and each had a golden crown on its head." And she led Eliza a short distance to where a little river wound its way between the trees.

Eliza said goodbye to the old woman and walked beside the river to the place where it opened out to the sea. She looked across the water but not one sail was to be seen. What was she to do now? She wandered along the pebbly shore and on the rough grass behind the pebbles she found eleven white swans' feathers. Drops of water lay on them, but whether they were dewdrops or tears she could not tell.

It was a lonely place, but strangely she did not feel alone for the sea was constantly changing. Then a great black cloud appeared, the wind blew and waves sprang up, as if the sea were saying, "I can be angry too." Then the cloud gleamed red, the wind dropped, and slowly the sun sank below the horizon in a blaze of crimson.

Just as the sun was about to set, Eliza saw eleven white swans with crowns on their heads flying towards the land, one after the other like a long white stream. She climbed over the bank behind the shore, hid herself and watched. The swans landed close to her and flapped and stretched their great wings. Then, just as the sun dropped beneath the water, their feathers fell off and eleven handsome princes, her brothers, stood there. With a loud cry she ran to them, calling their names. For although they were greatly changed she knew they must be her brothers. The princes were delighted to see their little sister and hugged her. They recognized her at once even though she was now a beautiful young woman. And they wept when they learned how cruel their stepmother had been.

Eliza's brothers told her that while the sun was shining they flew about as wild swans, but as soon as the sun sank they became human again. ''We have to be certain that we have somewhere to land when night falls, otherwise we should drop into the sea. We live in a land far across this sea. We can only visit our homeland once a year as we need two of the longest days to reach here, and then we have to spend the night on a little rock in the middle of the ocean, huddled close together while the spray splashes over us. We can stay here for eleven days and see the place where we were born, and visit the woods and rivers where we used to play. And here we have found you, Eliza, our little sister. How can we take you with us, for we have no boat?''

But Eliza only wanted to know how she could release them from the spell.

All night long they talked and talked, until at last they slept. In the morning Eliza heard the beating of swans' wings and saw her brothers flying overhead; only the youngest remained. She stroked his wings and they stayed together all day. Towards evening the others returned and when the sun had gone down they stood before her as princes again.

''Tomorrow we must fly away from here, and we cannot come back again for a whole year. But we cannot leave you behind. Are you brave enough to come with us? Surely our wings are strong enough to carry you.''

''Yes, please take me with you,'' she replied.

The whole night was spent weaving a net from reeds and just before dawn Eliza lay down on it. When the sun rose, her brothers seized the net in their beaks and flew with their sister high up towards the clouds. They flew so high that the large ships sailing beneath them looked like white seagulls on the shimmering sea.

Because the brothers were carrying the extra weight of their sister, their flight was slower than usual. Black clouds began to gather and evening drew near. Eliza looked anxiously at the setting sun, for the tiny, lonely rock could not yet be seen. She knew that she was the reason they were not flying fast enough.

When the sun sank below the sea her brothers would become men and they would all fall into the ocean and drown. The black clouds came nearer, lightning flashed and rain beat down upon them.

Now the sun was touching the edge of the water. Eliza's heart beat harder. Then the swans darted down so fast it seemed as if they were falling. The sun was already half hidden. And now, for the first time, Eliza saw the little rock beneath them. It was so small it looked as if a seal had thrust his head out of the water. The sun was sinking fast – now it was only a gleam above the surface of the sea. And then she felt land beneath her. Her brothers were standing round her, their arms around each other for there was only just enough room for them all. And so they spent the night, while the spray dashed over them and peal after peal of thunder rolled round them.

In the morning, as soon as the sun rose once more, the swans flew away with their sister from the island. And when she looked down, the sea was covered with white sea horses swimming upon the water.

At last, Eliza saw land with blue mountains, forests, cities and shining palaces. Long before the sun set, she was sitting on a rock in front of a large cave overhung with trailing green plants.

"Come and see where you will dream tonight," said her youngest brother, leading her inside the cave.

"Pray to God that I may dream of a way to free you from the spell," she replied. As she lay down she continued to pray and it seemed as if even while she was asleep she was still praying. For she was flying above the clouds to a fairy palace and when the fairy came out to greet her it was none other than the old woman she had met in the woods who had told her of the swans with crowns on their heads.

"Yes, your brothers can be released," she said. "But you will need great strength and courage, for you will have to endure much pain and suffering. Do you see this stinging nettle I am holding? There are many of them growing around the cave. You may use only those and the ones that grow in the churchyard. You must pick them, even though your hands will burn with blisters. Trample the nettles to pieces with your feet and you will have flax. With this flax you must weave eleven shirts with long sleeves which you must throw over the swans and the spell will be broken. But remember this – from the moment you begin this work until you have finished you must not speak. If one word passes your lips it will pierce your brothers' hearts like a dagger."

And she touched Eliza's hand with the nettle. It burned like fire and she awoke with the pain. It was broad daylight and close by she could see a nettle just like the one the old woman had held in the dream. She went out of the cave to begin her work. As she picked the coarse nettles great blisters came up on her hands and arms.

Then she bruised the nettles with her bare feet. They stung like fire, but she was determined to bear the pain if her brothers could be released.

When the nettles were broken into fibres she began to plait the green flax. At sunset her brothers returned and when they found she could not speak they were frightened and thought at first a new spell had been put on her. But they saw her blisters and with signs she indicated what she was doing, and they knew it was for them. The youngest brother wept and his tears fell on the ugly blisters. Eliza felt no more pain and the blisters disappeared.

All night she worked and the whole of the following day for she wanted to finish the shirts as quickly as possible. She finished one shirt and started on the second. Then she heard a hunting horn in the hills. A dog came bounding into the cave, followed by another, and another. Eliza gathered up her shirts and her nettles and sat herself on the bundle. The dogs started to bark and in a moment a group of huntsmen was at the opening of the cave. The tallest and handsomest came forward. He was the king of that country and never before had he seen such a beautiful young woman.

"Who are you? Where have you come from?" he asked.

Eliza shook her head. She could not answer him: it would cost her brothers their lives. And she hid her blistered hands under her apron.

"You must come with me," he said. "You cannot stay here all alone." And although she wept and tried to prevent them, she was lifted on to the king's horse. "I only want you to be happy," said the king. "You shall be dressed in soft silks and you shall sleep in a fine bed, not on a cave floor." Then he galloped off towards the mountains with Eliza on his horse.

They arrived at the castle where fountains played and within

the walls were lovely gardens with lily ponds and sweet scented flowers. But Eliza only wept and grieved for her brothers. Silently, she allowed the women to dress her in fine silks and to pull soft white gloves over her blistered hands.

When she stood before the king, dazzlingly beautiful, but with such sadness in her eyes, he loved her more than ever and chose her to be his bride, although the archbishop frowned and shook his head and whispered that the lovely girl was almost certainly a witch.

But the king paid no attention to such foolish ideas and ordered music to be played and a feast to be prepared. He led Eliza through the gardens to the halls. Later, he showed her where she was to sleep. A small room had been hung with green tapestries of woodland scenes. On the floor lay the bundle of flax which she had prepared from the nettles and from the ceiling hung the one completed shirt.

"Here you are," said the king. "A huntsman brought them from the cave. Perhaps you will be happier with these familiar things around you." For the first time Eliza smiled and pinkness came to her cheeks. She thought of the day when her brothers would be free and kissed the king's hand.

The king was determined she should be his queen. The marriage was announced and all the bells in the city rang with joy. The archbishop was to place the crown on Eliza's head. Her eyes glowed with love for the king, her new husband, but she could not speak. One word would cost her brothers their lives. If only she had been able to tell him the whole story. But she was compelled to remain dumb and finish her work in silence. At night she crept away from his side and went to the little room and wove her flaxen shirts. She finished six shirts and had started on the seventh when she had no flax left.

She knew that nettles grew on graves in the churchyard. She could use those. But how could she go there alone?

One night she crept out of the castle, through the deserted streets to the churchyard. She gathered as many of the fiery nettles as she could carry and took them back to her little room. Only one person saw her – the archbishop. Now he was convinced she was a witch, and that she had bewitched the king and all the people. He told the king what he had seen and what he believed. The king shook his head, but two heavy tears rolled down his cheeks. That night he lay awake and saw Eliza get up and disappear down the long corridor to her little room. Every night

she did this and the king grew more and more concerned. Was the archbishop right?

Now Eliza had only one shirt to complete, but the flax was finished. Once again she must make that frightening journey to the churchyard to gather a few handfuls of nettles. But this time the king and the archbishop followed her. They saw her go into the churchyard and begin to gather the nettles. "Only a witch would choose to gather nettles at night," thought the king.

Eliza was condemned to be burnt. She was led out of the beautiful halls and put in a bare cell. Instead of soft silks, she was given her nettles and instead of a coverlet she was given the ten shirts she had finished. But nothing could have pleased her more: she started to finish the eleventh shirt.

As evening approached she heard the whirring of wings close to the bars at the window. It was her brothers. They had found her and she cried for joy, even though she knew she was to be burnt the next day. The archbishop was sent to be with her, but she shook her head and persuaded him to leave by gently pushing him towards the door. Tonight was her last night and she knew she must finish her last shirt. The archbishop left, muttering evil words against her.

Just before dawn, the eleven brothers stood at the castle gates and demanded to see the king. "The king is asleep," they were told. They begged that he be woken up, but he was not to be disturbed. At last the king came to the gates to see these young men for himself. At that moment the sun rose and the brothers were no longer to be seen – only eleven wild swans flying over the castle.

The people came flocking to see their queen burnt as a witch. She was drawn through the streets on a cart. At her feet lay the ten completed shirts and even on her way to her death she continued to work on the eleventh. As she worked, she prayed.

"Look at her! She is muttering curses!" the mob shouted. And they pressed close to the cart. "Tear up her evil spells," they cried and tried to get at the shirts. At that, eleven wild swans appeared and sat round Eliza on the cart and beat off the people with their strong wings.

"It is a sign from heaven," whispered the people to each other. "She is certainly innocent." But they dared not say it aloud.

The executioner took her by the hand to lead her to the scaffold. She stood up and threw the eleven shirts over the swans as they stood on the sides of the cart. At once, eleven handsome princes stood there. But the shirt of the youngest had only one sleeve and he had a swan's wing instead of an arm.

"At last I may speak," she said. "I am innocent." Then she sank into her brothers' arms, with her eyes closed.

"Yes, she is innocent," said her brothers. Then the eldest brother told what had happened and as he told the story there was a wonderful smell of roses and every piece of wood that had been piled up for the fire sent out a shoot. A great hedge stood there, covered with bright red roses. But at the top was a single white flower. This the king picked and placed on Eliza's breast, and she awoke with love and happiness in her heart.

The church bells rang and back to the castle went the king with his lovely queen, Eliza.

THE PRINCESS AND THE PEA

Once upon a time there was a prince who wanted to marry a princess, but she would have to be a *real* princess. The prince went right round the world, and although he found several beautiful princesses, there was always something not quite right about them. So the prince came home again, very disappointed.

One night there was a terrible storm; it thundered, it lightninged and the rain came down in torrents. Suddenly there was a ringing of the bell at the palace gates. The king himself went to see who could be outside on such a dreadful night.

Outside there stood a princess. At least she said she was a princess. But what a sight she was! Water streamed off the ends of her long hair, ran down her clothes and into her shoes. The king told her to come in and she stood in front of the fire, dripping, and not looking at all like a princess.

"Yes, I am a princess," she assured them.

The old queen was doubtful and without saying a word she went to the spare bedroom. She took all the bedding off the bed and laid a pea at the bottom. Then she laid twenty mattresses on top of the pea and twenty feather beds on top of the mattresses. Here the princess was invited to spend the night.

The next morning the king asked the princess how she had slept.

"Oh, terribly badly. I hardly slept a wink all night. Goodness knows what was in the bed, but I was lying on something hard. I am black and blue all over!"

Now they knew she was a real princess. For no one but a princess would be able to feel a pea through twenty mattresses and twenty feather beds!

So the prince married her, for his search was at an end.

As for the pea, it was put into a museum where it may still be seen if no one has stolen it.

THE UGLY DUCKLING

✣

It was summer, glorious summer. The hay was in stacks in the meadows, the cornfields were turning yellow, the stork walked about on his long red legs while his young ones thought about flying from their untidy nest. In the middle of the sunshine was an old farm with red roofs surrounded by deep canals and from the farm wall down to the water grew huge burdocks, so high that children could stand upright underneath them. Here sat a mother duck upon her nest waiting for her eggs to hatch.

At last – "Piep! piep!" the eggs cracked and little creatures stuck their heads out. One by one the ducklings came out, quacking and gazing around. "How big the world is!" they exclaimed, for indeed it was much bigger than their world inside an egg.

"Do you think this is all the world?" asked their mother. "It is far bigger than this – it stretches right across the garden to the parson's field, but I have never been there. Now, are you all here?" And she stood up. "No, the biggest egg is still there. I wish it would hurry up for I am weary of it." She sat down again.

"How's it going?" asked an old duck who was passing.

"There's one egg that will not hatch," said the mother. "Look at the others, are they not the prettiest ducklings you ever saw?" And she looked fondly at her brood.

"Let me see the egg that will not hatch," said the old duck.

"Believe me, that's a turkey egg. Once I was cheated like that and I had so much trouble with the young ones. They would not go into the water, no matter how much I clucked. Yes, that's definitely a turkey egg. Leave it and teach your other children to swim."

"I think I will sit just a little longer," said the mother duck.

"As you please," said the old duck, going on her way.

At last the egg burst. "Piep! piep!" said the little one. It was very big and ugly. The duck looked at it.

"That's a very large duckling. It doesn't look like any of the others. Could it really be a turkey chick? Well, we shall soon find out. Into the water he shall go along with the rest, if I have to push him myself." And the mother duck went down to the canal with her little ones. Splash! One after another the ducklings plumped into the water after her. And the ugly grey duckling swam best of all.

"No, it's not a turkey," she said. "Look how well it uses its legs and how it holds its neck upright. On the whole it's not bad looking if you look at it properly. Quack! Quack! Come along: I'll take you to the farmyard, but keep close to me so that you don't get trodden on, and look out for the cats."

And so they went into the farmyard. There was a terrible fuss going on, for two families were quarrelling over an eel's head, but the cat got it in the end.

"That's the way of the world," said the mother duck. "Now walk straight and bow before the old duck over there. She is the grandest of all and has Spanish blood – that's why she's so fat – and do you see the red rag round her leg? That shows how distinguished she is. Now shake your feathers. Turn your toes out – a well brought up duck always turns its toes out – just as I do. Now bow your heads and say 'Quack'."

And so they did. But the others ducks in the farmyard looked at them and said, "What have we here? As if there weren't enough ducks around already. And just look at that one: we can't have one looking like that!" And one duck flew over and bit the duckling in the neck.

"Leave it alone," said the mother duck. "It's not doing any harm."

"Yes, but it's too big and peculiar," said the duck who had bitten it.

"Those are very pretty children you have," said the old duck with the rag round her leg. "All except one – it's a pity you can't change it."

"I'm afraid that cannot be done, Your Ladyship," said the mother duck. "It may not be pretty, but it has a very nice nature and swims better than any of the others. I think it was in the egg too long and therefore is rather an odd shape." And she stroked the duckling's neck and smoothed its feathers. "Anyway, it's a drake," she said, "so it doesn't matter so much. I think he will be very strong one day."

"Well, make yourself at home," said the old duck. "And if you

find an eel's head you may bring it to me."

And so they were at home, but the duckling who had come last out of the egg was pushed and pulled and pecked and kicked until even its brothers and sisters were angry with it and said, "If only the cat would catch you, you ugly thing!" And the girl who came to feed the birds in the poultry yard kicked it with her foot, until at last one day it was so terrified it ran and flew over the wall. Then it ran and ran until it came to the moor where the wild ducks lived. There it lay the whole night through, lonely and miserable.

In the morning the wild ducks came up and looked at their new companion.

"You're remarkably ugly," they said. "I hope you don't marry into our family." But the duckling had no intention of marrying and only wanted to stay among the reeds.

One day, two wild geese were passing by. "You can come with us if you want," they said. "Nearby on another moor there are several wild geese, all unmarried. You might make your fortune there." Bang! bang! sounded in the air and the two geese fell down dead in the swamp. The water turned red and whole flocks of geese rose up from the reeds. Bang! bang! sounded again. There was a great hunt on and the swamp was surrounded by men with guns. Dogs came splashing through, bending the reeds on all sides. The duckling was terrified and hid its head under its wing, but at that moment a great hairy dog stood in front of it, his red tongue hanging out and his eyes gleaming. He pushed his nose in the duckling's face, and then splash! splash! went on his way without touching it.

"I am so ugly," the duckling thought, "that even the dog doesn't want to bite me." It lay quite still, too terrified to move until the hunters had gone. It waited a long time and then hurried away from the moor as fast as it could. It ran on over the fields through a terrible storm until it came to a dilapidated little hut. The duckling tried to shelter from the storm behind the hut, but it was so old and creaky that the wind whistled round the duckling until it was forced to sit down. Then the duckling noticed that the door was not hanging properly on its hinges, so it slipped through a crack into the hut.

In the hut lived an old woman with her hen and her cat. The cat was called Sonny. He could arch his back and purr and if you stroked his fur the wrong way he gave out sparks. The hen had short little legs and was called Chickabiddy-shortshanks. But she laid good eggs and the old woman loved her.

The next morning the hen and cat noticed the duckling immediately. The cat began to purr and the hen to cluck. The old woman was rather shortsighted and looked all around. She thought the duckling was a fat duck that had strayed away from home. "This is splendid," she said. "Now we shall have duck's eggs.

I hope it is not a drake.''

And so the duckling was allowed to stay for three weeks, but no eggs came. The hen and the cat thought they were half the world and the better half at that and lorded it over the duckling.

"Can you lay eggs?" asked the hen.

"No."

"Then hold your tongue."

"Can you arch your back and purr and give out sparks?" asked the cat.

"No."

"Then don't interrupt when sensible people are speaking."

And the duckling sat in a corner and fell silent.

Then the sunshine streamed through a crack in the walls and it was seized with such a longing to swim that it could not help telling the hen about it.

"What are you talking about?" cried the hen. "You have nothing to do, that's why you have these strange ideas. Purr or lay eggs and they'll soon go away."

"But it is so wonderful to swim on the water, to dive down to the bottom and let the waters close over one."

"I suppose that might be quite pleasant," said the hen. "But you had better ask the cat. He's the cleverest animal I know. Ask him if

he likes to swim on the water and dive down to the bottom. Or ask our mistress, the old woman; there's no one cleverer than she. Do you suppose she would like to swim and let the waters close over her head?"

"You don't understand," said the duckling.

"I don't understand!" said the hen. "Are you telling me that you are cleverer than the cat and the old woman? I won't speak for myself. Don't be ridiculous and be grateful for all the kindness you have received. Haven't you had warmth and friendship? I'm only speaking for your own good. Nobody likes hearing unpleasant things, but that's the only way to find who one's real friends are. Just take care that you learn to lay eggs and to purr and give out sparks!"

"I think I will go out into the wide world," said the duckling.

"Yes, just go," said the hen.

And so the duckling went away. It swam on the water and dived, but every creature it met ignored it.

Autumn came and the weather grew colder. The leaves began to fall and the wind caught them and they danced about. The clouds hung low, heavy with rain, and the crows stood on the fence saying, "Craaak! Craaak!" One evening, just as the sun was setting, a whole flock of handsome birds flew over the trees. They were swans with long necks, dazzling white, and as they flew they uttered strange cries. The little duckling watched them flying overhead to warmer lands, to open water. How it longed to be like them. It turned round and round in the water, making such strange noises it frightened itself. It did not know what the birds were, nor where they were going, but it loved them more than it had ever loved anything before.

Then came the winter. The duckling was obliged to swim about in the water to stop itself from freezing, but every night the hole where it was swimming became smaller and smaller. At last it froze so hard that the duckling was completely trapped in the ice.

The next morning a workman passed by and saw what had happened. He took off his boot, broke the ice and carried the duckling home. There it revived and the children wanted to play with it. But the duckling thought they might hurt it, so it flew up and knocked down the milk pan. The mother clapped her hands which frightened the duckling and it fluttered down into the butter churn and then into the flour barrel. The mother yelled and hit out with the tongs, the children fell over each other trying to catch the duckling and there was a fine to-do. Luckily the door was slightly open and the duckling slipped outside, where it lay exhausted in the newly fallen snow.

All through the winter the duckling endured the cold among the reeds, but at last the sun began to shine again, the larks to sing. Spring had arrived.

The duckling flapped its wings: they felt stronger than before and it flew up and away to a large park where apple trees were flowering. In the middle was a great lake where three glorious white swans were swimming. The duckling recognized the splendid creatures and felt strangely sad.

''I will go to them and they will kill me because I am so ugly. But better to be killed by such beautiful creatures than to be pecked by ducks, kicked by the girl who feeds the poultry, chased by children and to suffer such terrible cold and hunger.'' It flew onto the water and swam towards the swans. They looked at the duckling and came sailing down the lake to it with outstretched wings.

''Kill me,'' said the duckling, bowing its head to the water. But what was this it saw? No ugly grey duckling looked up from the surface, but a beautiful white swan!

It doesn't matter if you are born in a farmyard if you come from a swan's egg.

The big swans swam round it stroking it with their beaks. Soon some little children came down to the lake with crusts of bread. "There's a new one!" they shouted. And they ran to tell their father and mother. "A new one has arrived. The new one is the most beautiful of all!"

He felt quite embarrassed and hid his head under his wing for he did not know what to do. He remembered how he had been teased and mocked and now he heard children saying that he was the most beautiful of all. Then he opened his wings and lifted his neck and cried out with joy from the depths of his heart, "I never dreamed of so much happiness when I was an ugly duckling!"

THE LITTLE MERMAID

✤

Far out at sea where the water is blue as blue and so deep that many tall steeples could be placed one on top of the other, there live the sea people.

The Sea King's castle is made of coral with tall towers. The roof is made of shells which open and shut with the flow of the water and in each shell lies a gleaming pearl. Surrounding the castle are many strange sea plants and among their stems swim shoals of fish of brilliant hues.

The Sea King's wife had died many years ago and now his old mother kept the house for him. She was very grand and wore twelve oysters on her tail, while other important people were only allowed to wear six. There were six little Sea Princesses and their grandmother was very fond of them. They were all lovely, but the youngest was the most beautiful: her skin was soft and clear, her eyes were blue as the deepest sea and like all the others she had no feet, for her body ended in a long fishtail.

All day long the princesses played in the castle; the great windows were open and fishes swam in and out. Outside the castle was a beautiful garden with fiery red corals and lovely fan corals, which grew just like bright red and blue flowers. A blue light lay everywhere and sometimes on calm days when the sun could be seen it looked like a great purple flower.

In the garden, each of the princesses had her own little corner where she could plant what she liked. Each one made her flower-bed a different shape and the older princesses arranged patterns out of things they had found on wrecked ships. But the youngest would have none of these things; she would only have red flowers growing in her garden which was in the shape of the sun, red flowers and a pretty marble statue of a boy, which had sunk down to the bottom of the sea. She planted a pink flowering tree beside the statue and the branches hung down over the ground, waving in the blue light.

The little princess loved to hear about the world of men above them. The grandmother had to tell all she knew about towns and cities and ships and people and animals. She was amazed that up above them the flowers had sweet scents and creatures like fishes could sing loudly and clearly among the trees. The grandmother said they were called birds.

"When you have your fifteenth birthday," said the grand-mother, "you shall rise up and sit on the rocks in the moonlight and see the great ships go sailing by. Then you will see cities and towns."

The following year the eldest sister would be fifteen years old; each of the others was one year younger than the next, so that the youngest sister had five years to wait before she could rise up from the bottom of the sea and see what the world looked like. But each one promised to tell the others what she had seen and what she thought most beautiful on her visit, for they were all longing to know what went on in the world above them. And none of them was more anxious than the youngest sister.

Often at night she would stand at the castle windows and look up through the dark blue water trying to see the moon and stars.

Sometimes a great black shape passed overhead and she knew it was either a whale or a ship filled with people, none of whom knew that there was a little mermaid deep down below stretching up her hands towards them.

At last it was the birthday of the eldest princess and she swam up to the surface of the sea.

When she came home she had hundreds of things to tell her sisters. But the best thing of all, she said, was to lie on a sandbank in the moonlight, listening to the waves and watching the lights twinkling in a nearby town and to hear music and church bells and the clatter of the wheels of the carriages. Oh, how the youngest longed for her fifteenth birthday!

The following year the second sister was given permission to swim up to the surface. She emerged just as the sun was setting; the whole sky seemed to be made of gold and the clouds were lit from behind with a golden light. A flight of white swans soared overhead. She swam towards them, but the sun sank below the horizon before she could reach them. It was the most beautiful thing she had ever seen, she told her sisters.

The next year the third sister went up. She boldly swam up a river that flowed into the sea. She saw green hills covered with vines; castles with turrets peeped out from woodland and the birds sang gaily all day. The sun was hot and she frequently had to dive beneath the water to cool her face. In a little bay she found a group of young humans splashing about in the water quite naked. She swam towards them, but they ran away in fright and a little black animal came down to the water's edge and barked and barked. She was frightened and swam back to the open sea. But she never forgot the green woods, the hills and the little children who could swim in the water even though they did not have fishtails.

The fourth sister was more timid. She stayed out in the open sea, floating on her back and lazily flipping her tail in the sunshine. She could see for miles and the sky above was just like a great bell. In the far distance were ships with white sails. Dolphins had swum around her, leaping out of the water and encouraging her to play with them.

Then it was the turn of the fifth sister. Her birthday was in the winter and she saw what the others did not see: the sea was icy green and great icebergs floated on the surface of the water. They were the strangest shapes and shone in the sunshine like diamonds. She sat upon one of the biggest of them and let the wind play with her long hair. She watched the sailing ships tack about in the distance and towards evening clouds covered the sky; great black waves lifted the icebergs high in the water, the ships took down their sails and the sailors prayed for their safety. She sat quietly on her floating iceberg watching flashes of lightning dart into the sea.

When she went up for the first time each of the sisters was

delighted with what she saw, but now that they were grown-up girls and could go up whenever they wished they quickly tired of their new-found freedom and after a short time decided that it was best of all down below, at home. But sometimes the five sisters took one another by the hand and rose up together over the water. There they sang lilting songs to the sailors, telling them not to be afraid for it was beautiful down below. But the sailors could not understand the words and thought it was the wind sighing and if their ship sank and they were drowned, they came to the Sea King's palace as corpses.

When her sisters went up together arm in arm, the youngest sister was left all alone and she felt like weeping. But mermaids have no tears.

At last she was really fifteen years old.

"Now it is your turn," said the old grandmother. "Come, let me dress you like your sisters."

She put a wreath of white shells and sea flowers in the young girl's hair and she allowed eight great oysters to attach themselves to the princess's tail.

"Oh, that hurts so!" exclaimed the princess.

"One must suffer to be beautiful," replied the old lady.

How glad the princess would have been to shake off the pinching oysters and to lay down the heavy wreath. She preferred the flowers in her garden, but she had to do as she was told. "Farewell," she said, and she rose like a bubble through the sea.

When she lifted her head above the waves the sun had just set but the clouds still shone with roses and gold. The sea was calm and the evening air was mild and balmy. A great ship with three masts lay in front of her, quite becalmed in the still air. There was music and singing and as darkness fell the whole ship blazed with lantern-light. The little mermaid swam close to the cabin windows and as the waves lifted her up she could see through the panes where many people all dressed in their best were laughing and talking. The handsomest of them all was a young prince with black hair and sparkling eyes; it was his sixteenth birthday and that was the reason for all the merriment.

On the deck the sailors were dancing and when the young prince came out more than a hundred fireworks shot up into the air. They startled the little mermaid who dived beneath the waves, but she soon put her head out again and then it seemed as if hundreds of stars were falling around her. She had never seen fireworks before. They leaped high above the ship in greens, reds, silvers and golds. Great suns spurted fire and fiery fishes flew over

the sea. The ship itself was sharply lit up and each separate rope could be seen. The little mermaid could see each person clearly and oh, how handsome the young prince was!

It grew late, but the princess could not turn her eyes away from the ship. The lanterns were put out, the music stopped and no more rockets were fired into the air. The mermaid floated on the water, peeping into the cabins. Then the sails were hoisted and the ship started on her way. But now the waves rose higher, great clouds rolled up and there was lightning in the distance. It was going to be a fearful night. The sailors took down the sails and the ship flew over the towering waves like a great bird. The mermaid followed, enjoying the storm. But the sailors feared for their lives. The ship groaned and creaked and the waves broke over the decks as if they would smash them.

Then the sea broke the ship: the mainmast snapped in two and the ship keeled over on her side while the waters rushed into the hold. Now the mermaid saw that the people were in danger; she herself had to be careful to avoid spars and planks and pieces of the ship that were floating around her. She looked especially for the young prince for she had seen him sink into the sea. She was glad, for now he would come down to her home beneath the waves. Then she remembered that people could not live beneath the water and that when he came to her father's palace he would certainly be dead. He must not die. She swam about among the debris of the ship that floated on the surface, searching for him. Down she dived beneath the waves, and again she rose, eagerly seeking him. At last she saw him, clinging to a piece of wood and nearly exhausted in the stormy sea. His legs failed him and his eyes closed. But the little mermaid was near; she held his head up and allowed the waves to carry them wherever they willed.

When morning came the storm had passed. Nothing was to be seen of the ship. The sun came up out of the water and it was as if its warmth brought some life to the cheeks of the young prince, but his eyes remained closed. The mermaid kissed his forehead and pushed back his wet hair and he seemed to her like the marble statue in her little garden. She kissed him again and willed him to live.

In front of her the mermaid saw high hills with snow-capped peaks. Up the sides of the hills rose green forests out of which peeped white turrets. And down the coast was a large building surrounded by white walls. In the gardens she could see lemon and orange trees and palms waved at the gates. There the sea formed a little bay surrounded by rocks and fine silver sand. Into the bay swam the mermaid with the handsome prince and laid

him gently on the warm sand. Then she swam out a little way and watched to see what would happen.

A bell rang in the building and a crowd of young girls came out into the garden; one of them came through the gates on to the strand and was very surprised to see the prince lying there. Quickly she ran back and brought several more people who surrounded the prince and helped him to stand up. He was led away through the gates of the building and the mermaid saw him no more. She dived sorrowfully through the waves and returned to her father's palace.

When her sisters asked her what she had seen she could tell them nothing, but only stayed sadly in her little garden gazing at her marble statue.

Often in the early evening she rose to the surface and swam to the bay where she had left the prince. She saw the fruits in the garden ripen and watched them being gathered. She saw the snow melt on the mountain, but she did not see the prince and she came home more sad than before and went out to her garden where she put her arms round her little statue and stayed there thinking of the prince.

At last, one day she told one of her sisters what had happened and she told the others, but nobody else knew; only the six sisters and a few other mermaids who were their closest friends. One of these knew who the prince was and where his kingdom lay. So one evening the six sisters joined hands and together they swam up to the place where the prince had his palace.

The palace was built of yellow stone with marble staircases and richly tiled turrets. One of the staircases led from a marble balcony right down to the sea. Now that the mermaid knew where he lived she spent many a night floating on the water gazing at the palace

and swimming under the splendid balcony where she could watch the young prince, who thought he was quite alone in the moonlight.

Sometimes she saw him sailing in his boat with his friends and listened to their singing. If anyone saw her silver veil they thought it was a swan spreading its wings. She saw how people loved him and remembered how his head had lain on her breast and how she had kissed him. But he knew nothing about her and could not even dream of her.

More and more she began to long to be able to wander about the land as people do. She envied the people their freedom, freedom to sail over the sea on ships, to climb the mountains and to walk in the fields and woods. There was so much she wanted to know, but when she asked her sisters they could not answer all her questions. So she asked the old grandmother: "If people do not drown, do they live for ever?"

"No, no," replied the grandmother. "They too must die, and their life is shorter than ours. We can live for three hundred years and when we die we become the salt sea foam. But when people die their soul goes to a heavenly kingdom far above the stars."

"Why cannot we go to a heavenly kingdom?" asked the little mermaid. "I would happily give up all the hundreds of years of life down here to be able to go to a heavenly kingdom when I die."

"You mustn't think like that," replied the old lady. "We are far happier and far better than the humans who walk on the land."

"Then am I to die and be turned into foam upon the sea? Is there nothing I can do to go to heaven?"

"No!" replied the grandmother. "Only if a man were to love you and want to marry you and spend the rest of his life with you. Then his soul would be planted in your body and you would have a share of his happiness. But it can never happen. Your fishtail, which we look upon as beautiful, is considered ugly in the world above. There, it is necessary to have two stilt-like supports called legs to be beautiful."

The little mermaid sighed and looked sadly at her long green fishtail.

"Come," said the old lady. "Let us have a court ball and dance and leap and sing."

It was wonderful: the walls and ceiling of the ballroom were made of clearest glass; hundreds of shells stood on either side filled with a blue fire which lit the hall and also lit up the sea so that it was possible to see all the fishes that swam up to the walls. Through the middle of the hall flowed a broad stream where the sea men and sea women danced. As they danced they sang and the little mermaid had the most lovely voice of them all. She felt happy for she knew her singing was sweeter and clearer than that of anybody else either in the sea or on the earth. And then she remembered the prince and her sadness at not having a soul like his. She slipped out of her father's palace and went to her little garden and sat sorrowfully listening to the laughter and merriment within. She heard a horn sound above her and thought to herself, "Now he is sailing up there, he with whom I should like to spend the rest of my life. I would do anything to win him. While my sisters are dancing I will go to the sea witch, even though I have always been afraid of her, and see if she can help me."

The little mermaid went out of her garden to make her way to the swirling whirlpools where the sea witch lived.

No flowers grew here, only dark seaweeds which stretched out their tendrils to catch her as she passed. The sand was dark grey and she had to cross warm, bubbling mud. This the witch called her turf moor. The house lay in the middle of a forest of strange creatures, which were half animal, half plant. All the branches were long slimy arms with fingers like worms which could curl round and trap whoever passed by. The little mermaid stopped in front of them, too terrified to go further. Then she thought of the prince and she tied up her long flying hair so that the creatures could not seize it, put her arms close to her sides and shot forward like a fish through the ugly creatures, who she saw were holding in their long fingers the limbs of people who had drowned at sea.

Now she came to a great marshy place in the middle of which was the sea witch's house, built from the bones of shipwrecked sailors. All around swam great sea snakes with cold eyes that looked hungrily at the pretty little mermaid. There sat the sea witch feeding her pet toad.

"I know what you want," she said, "you silly little thing. You want me to help you to get rid of your fishtail and have two ugly supports instead, so that the prince will fall in love with you and you will go to heaven. Well, I will do what you want, but it will only bring you unhappiness and grief." The witch laughed out loud and the toad fell to the ground. "You are just in time," she continued. "After tomorrow I could not have helped you until another year had passed. I will give you a potion. With this you must swim to land, sit yourself down and drink it. Your tail will shrivel and you will have two legs like the people of the earth. You will walk gracefully and elegantly and no woman will dance more beautifully, but every step you take will be like walking on sharp knives. If you think you can bear this, I will help you."

The little mermaid trembled, but she thought of the prince and she whispered a soft "Yes" to the witch.

"There is something else," said the witch. "Once you have lost your tail and become a human, you can never be a mermaid again. You can never come back to your father's palace and to your sisters. If you do not win the prince's love so that he wants to marry you and live with you for the rest of his life, you will not go to heaven. The first morning after he has married someone else, your heart will break and you will become foam on the water."

"I will do it," said the little mermaid, trembling.

"But you must pay me," said the witch. "I must have payment for my potion. You have the sweetest voice of all in the sea, but this voice you must give to me."

"But if you take away my voice, what will I have left?" said the little mermaid.

"You will have your beauty, your graceful walk, your lovely eyes. What more do you want? Have you lost your courage? Put out your tongue so that I may cut it off for payment, then you shall have the potion."

"All right, you shall have it," said the little mermaid.

The witch got out her pot to prepare the potion. "Cleanliness is a good thing," she said, as she scrubbed out the pot with snakes which she had tied up in a big knot. She scratched herself and let the drops of blood fall into the pot. She threw in all manner of things and the pot boiled and bubbled and the steam rose up in the strangest shapes. At last the potion was ready and looked like pure, clear water.

Then the witch cut off the mermaid's tongue so that she could neither speak nor sing.

She could see her father's palace. The ball was over, the lights were out and they were surely asleep, but she could not go to them to say goodbye, for she could not speak. She slipped into the garden and took one flower from each of her sisters' beds, blew a hundred kisses towards the palace and then rose up through the dark blue sea.

The sun was not yet up when she came to the prince's palace and climbed the marble staircase. She reached the balcony and drank the witch's potion. It was as if a fiery sword went through her body and she fell down in a faint. When she awoke the sun was shining down over the sea and standing in front of her was the handsome prince. She glanced down and saw that her fishtail was gone and that she had a pair of white feet and long slender legs. But she had no clothes on and she covered herself with her shining hair.

The prince asked her who she was and how she came to be there. But she could not answer him. He took her hand and led her into the castle and every step she took was as if she was walking on sharp knives. By his side she walked as light as a bubble and everyone was astonished at her beauty.

She was given clothes of flowing silk and was the most beautiful person in the whole castle, but she was dumb and could neither speak nor sing. When she heard other young girls sing before the court she was sad, for she knew that she could have sung far more sweetly. "Oh, if only he knew," she thought, "that I gave away my voice to be with him!"

When she danced, she danced as no one had danced before. The prince was enchanted and called her his little foundling, so she danced for him again, but each time her feet touched the floor it felt as if she were dancing on knives. The prince had a page's outfit made for her and she rode with him through the green woods and climbed the high mountains, even though her delicate feet bled, but she laughed and followed him higher and higher until they were above the clouds.

At night when everyone in the castle was asleep she went out onto the marble balcony and descended the marble steps to the sea. There she cooled her burning feet in the cold sea water and thought of her family in the deep. One night her sisters came hand in hand looking for her. She beckoned to them and they came closer and told her how sad and empty the court was without her. After that they came to her every night and once in the distance she spied her old grandmother who had not been up to the surface for many a long year. Even the Sea King himself, his crown upon his head, came to see his youngest daughter, but he did not dare venture too near the land.

As the days went by, the prince grew more and more fond of her. He loved her as a father loves his daughter; it never entered his head that he might marry her. He kissed her and stroked her hair. "You remind me of a maiden I once saw who rescued me from a storm. She is the only one in the whole world whom I

'could truly love, but I shall never see her again,'' he said.

"He does not know that I am that one, the one who saved his life,'' thought the little mermaid. ''I carried him over the sea to safety and now I am with him every day. I will love him and cherish him and even die for him.''

Then it was announced that the prince was to marry the beautiful daughter of a king whose lands lay not far away. A ship was being prepared and on this the prince was to sail over the sea to bring his bride home.

"I must travel,'' the prince said to the mermaid. ''I have to see this princess. My parents wish it, but I am not forced to marry her. If I could choose, I would rather marry you, my little foundling with the speaking eyes. But you must accompany me on the voyage. That I insist on.'' And he kissed her and played with her long hair. The little mermaid dreamed of happiness and of going to a heavenly kingdom.

As the prince and the little mermaid stood together on the deck of the ship that was carrying them to the kingdom of the princess, she listened to his stories of storms and calm, of strange fishes in the deep and of what divers had seen. She smiled to herself, for no one knew better than she what happened at the bottom of the sea.

When the ship sailed into the port of the king's city all the church bells rang out and from high towers trumpets sounded. Every day there were balls and concerts, but the prince had to wait for the princess to arrive. At last she came.

The little mermaid was anxious to see her. Would she be beautiful? Would she be gracious? Could she sing and dance? When she saw the princess she acknowledged that she was both beautiful and gracious – her dark blue eyes shone behind long dark eyelashes, her skin was clear and lovely and her smile was radiant.

"It is you!" cried the prince. "You are the one who saved me when I lay for dead upon the shore." He turned to the little mermaid. "I am so happy! Be happy for me, for you are more devoted to me than anyone." And he clasped the princess to his heart.

The little mermaid kissed his hand, and it seemed as if her heart were already broken for on the morning after his wedding she would be only foam upon the sea.

The church bells began to ring and heralds rode through the streets announcing the engagement of the princess to the handsome prince. On the day of the wedding the little mermaid was dressed in a golden gown and held up the bride's train, but her eyes saw nothing of the splendid ceremony, her ears did not hear the swelling music; she thought only of the night and of her coming death and all she had lost.

That evening the prince and his bride went on board ship; they were to spend their honeymoon sailing across the sunlit seas. In the middle of the ship a tent of gold had been prepared where a bed covered with silk cushions had been laid. Here the royal couple were to sleep.

The wind filled the sails and the ship glided smoothly away from the dockside and out to sea. When it grew dark, lamps were lit and the sailors danced on deck. The little mermaid thought of the first time she had seen the prince when all were dancing to celebrate his birthday. Now she joined in the dancing for his wedding and all who saw her admired her grace and beauty. Although every step she took cut her feet as if with knives, she did not feel the pain: her heart was far more bitterly wounded. She knew this was the last evening she would be alive to see him, he for whom she had given up so much. She had left her home, lost her beautiful voice, and suffered terrible pain every day, but he was quite unaware of it all. Everyone was full of gladness and joy tonight. The prince kissed his bride and together they went to rest in their splendid tent.

Now the ship was quiet; only the helmsman stood at the helm. The little mermaid leant her arms on the ship's side and looked towards the east for the dawn – she knew the first ray of the sun would kill her. Then she saw her sisters rise from the depths. Their long beautiful hair no longer floated behind them; it had been cut off.

"We gave it to the sea witch, so that you may not die tonight," they said. "She has given us a knife – look how sharp it is – before the sun rises you must plunge it into the prince's heart. When his warm blood falls on your feet they will grow together again into a fishtail and you will again be a mermaid and come back to us and live your three hundred years. Hurry! Either you or he must die before sunrise. Kill the prince and come back! Do you see those red lights in the sky? The sun is just coming up – in a few minutes you will die." And they sighed and sank back beneath the waves.

The little mermaid drew back the silk curtain of the tent and saw the prince and his bride sleeping peacefully on the silken cushions. She bent down and kissed his forehead. Then she looked up and saw the sky getting brighter and brighter. She looked at the knife in her hands, glanced again at the prince and turned and flung the knife far into the waves which seemed to spurt drops of blood as the knife fell. Then the mermaid threw herself from the ship into the sea and felt herself dissolving into foam.

Now the sun rose out of the sea. The warm rays fell on the cold sea foam, and the little mermaid felt nothing of death. She looked up and saw over her head hundreds of glorious creatures floating through the air. She found herself being drawn up out of the foam to join them. "Where am I going?" she asked.

"To the daughters of the air," they replied. "You have suffered so much, but after three hundred years you can win an immortal soul."

The little mermaid lifted her eyes to the sun and for the first time felt them fill with tears. On the ship below she could see the prince and his bride looking for her; they looked over the side at the salt sea foam as if they knew she had thrown herself into the waves. Then with the other children of the air she floated higher and higher, towards heaven.

THE LITTLE MATCH GIRL

It was the last day of the year and terribly cold. A little girl with bare feet was walking slowly along the freezing street. When she had left her house she had been wearing slippers, but they were

far too large for her as they had belonged to her mother. They fell off as she slipped across the road to avoid two carriages that went rattling by terribly fast. One slipper was lost completely and a little boy had picked up the other and run off with it: he thought perhaps he could use it as a cradle when he had children of his own. So now she had nothing on her feet at all. In her old apron she carried bundles of matches, for she was a match girl, but no one had bought anything from her all day. No one had given her even a farthing.

She crept along, trying to keep in the shelter of the walls of the houses from which came the most wonderful smell of roast goose. Snow fell on her fair hair as she sat down in a corner beside two houses where one jutted out beyond the other. She tucked her feet under her as well as she could for it was bitterly cold and she did not dare to go home as she had earned no money, and her father would certainly beat her. It was just as cold at home for they had no fire and the wind whistled through the holes in the roof.

Her hands were stiff with the cold – perhaps if she struck a match it would warm them a little. She drew out one of her bundles and scraped a match against the wall. Sc-r-ritch! It spat and burned brightly. When she held her hands over it, it seemed as if she was sitting in front of a big stove, with brass feet. How warm and cosy the fire was. But the little flame went out and the stove vanished. In her hands she had only the end of the match.

She scraped a second match against the wall. It blazed and its light shone on the wall which became transparent. She could see through it into the room where a table was laid with a fine white cloth. On it stood a shining dinner service with a roast goose stuffed with apples and prunes. Then the goose hopped off the dish, with the knife and fork sticking out, and came towards the little girl. The match went out and she was staring at the cold, damp wall.

She lit another. This time she was sitting under a beautiful Christmas tree, bigger and more splendid even than the one she had seen through the doors of the rich man's house. Hundreds of candles burned upon the green branches and toys dangled from the boughs. She stretched out her hand towards them, but the match went out.

Now the candles seemed to burn as stars in the sky. As she watched, one of them fell to earth, leaving a long tail of fire. "Somebody is dying," she thought, for her old grandmother, who was now dead, had once told her that when a star fell down, a soul went up to God.

She rubbed another match against the wall and this time she saw the old grandmother herself, smiling and soft and lovely.

"Grandmother!" she cried. "Take me with you. Hurry, before you vanish like the warm stove and the roast goose and the Christmas tree!"

Quickly the little girl rubbed the whole bundle of matches

against the wall, and there was the grandmother more beautiful than ever. The light was as bright as day. The grandmother took the little girl in her arms and together they flew high up above the earth to where there is no hunger or cold or pain. They were with God.

The little girl was found the next day, frozen to death as she sat against the wall, with a smile on her frozen lips. Beside her lay the bundle of matches, all-burned down to nothing.

"She tried to warm herself, poor little thing," they said to each other. But none of them knew what glorious things she had seen and with what joy she had gone to join her grandmother.

THE SNOW QUEEN

A STORY IN SEVEN CHAPTERS

The First Chapter

THE MIRROR AND ITS FRAGMENTS

Once there was a very bad goblin, one of the worst kind, in fact he was a demon. One day he was particularly pleased with himself for he had made a mirror, a very unusual mirror. Anything good or beautiful reflected in it shrank away almost to nothing, and anything bad or ugly stood out more than ever. The most lovely views looked like boiled cabbage and the nicest people turned hideous. The demon thought this very funny. He showed the mirror to his friends at the goblin school and they had the idea of flying up to heaven with the mirror to show it to the angels. What fun that would be! Higher and higher they flew with the mirror and the higher they got the more the mirror grinned to itself. Suddenly the mirror started to tremble, it was grinning so hard, and then the trembling was so strong that the mirror broke into millions and millions of tiny pieces, some of them so small they could scarcely be seen.

But now the mirror caused much more unhappiness than

before, for if one of these tiny fragments flew into anyone's eye it stuck there, and that person only saw the bad side of everything: they saw nothing good or beautiful at all. A few people even got little pieces of mirror in their hearts and that was the worst of all, for their hearts turned into lumps of ice. Some pieces of the mirror were large enough to make into window panes or spectacles. It was not a good idea to look at the world through these; but the demon just laughed and laughed. And some little fragments were still floating around the world . . .

The Second Chapter

A LITTLE BOY AND A LITTLE GIRL

In a big town two children lived opposite one another in two little garrets. The houses in the street were high and leaned over towards each other so that at the very top it was possible to step from one little garret to another without running down all the stairs.

The parents of each child had a large box in which they grew herbs to be used in cooking and they also grew rose bushes, one in each box. The roses grew well and in summer the bushes were covered with flowers. Sometimes the children took their stools and sat out on the roof in the shade of the roses, where they could play together.

But in winter it was not possible to play like that. The windows were often quite frozen over and the children took pennies and warmed them on the stove. Then they held the warm coins against the frozen panes and made a round peep-hole and behind each peep-hole gleamed a little eye! These eyes belonged to the little boy and the little girl. He was called Kay and she was called Gerda. Now that it was winter, when they wanted to play together they had to go down and up the long staircases, while outside the snow came tumbling.

"It is white bees swarming," said the old grandmother.

"Do they have a queen?" asked Kay, for he knew that real bees

always have a queen.

"Oh, yes," replied the grandmother. "She is the largest of them all and flies about the town at night looking in all the windows. When the windows freeze they look like flowers."

"Oh, I've seen that!" both children cried.

"Could the Snow Queen come in here?" asked little Gerda.

"Just let her try," cried Kay. "I would put her upon the stove, and then she'd melt!"

The grandmother stroked his hair and told them another story.

Later, when Kay was back at home and ready for bed, he climbed on a chair by the window and peeped out through the little hole. A few snowflakes were falling and one of them, larger than all the others, was lying on the edge of one of the flower boxes. It grew larger and larger and at last became a snow maiden, beautiful and delicate, made of starry crystals. She nodded to little Kay and beckoned with her icy finger. But he was frightened and jumped off the chair, and then it seemed as if a great bird flew past the window.

The next day was sparkling with frost, and then spring came: the snow melted, the swallows arrived and built their nests and soon it was summer – glorious, flowering summer. Kay and Gerda sat out in their little garden high up on the roof, looking at their picture book. Then, one day, just as the church clock struck twelve, Kay said, "Oh! Something flew into my eye and pricked my heart!"

The little girl hugged him. He blinked his eyes and said, "I think it's gone." But it was not gone. It was one of those tiny fragments of glass from the magic mirror, the mirror that made everything good and beautiful seem mean and ugly. Poor Kay also had a splinter in his heart. It did not hurt him, but his heart would soon be like a lump of ice.

"What are you crying for?" he said. "How ugly you are! And look at that rose – it's all worm-eaten and horrible. Why do we have the stupid roses anyway?" And he tore off the flowers and kicked the box.

"Kay! What are you doing?" cried Gerda.

He jumped away from her and in at his own window. Gerda followed him with the picture book, but he said it was babyish and he was fed up with it. Now, when the old grandmother told them stories, he always argued and mimicked her behind her back. He followed people in the street, copying them, and he teased little Gerda who loved him dearly.

One winter's day he came in with his sled on his back and called up the stairs to Gerda that he was going to play in the square with the other boys.

In the square boys sometimes tied their sleds to people's carts and when the cart moved off they had a good ride. While the boys were playing, a great white sleigh came into the square and drove round it twice. The driver was wrapped in rough white fur with a fur cap on his head. Kay tied his little sled to the white sleigh and was pulled round the square with it. Faster and faster they went through the white streets. The driver turned round and nodded to Kay as if they knew each other. Kay would have liked to cut himself loose, but the man turned round again and nodded. Now they were outside the gates of the town and snow began to fall, so thickly that the boy could not see where they were going. If only he could cut himself free, but it was quite impossible for they were going like the wind. He shouted to the man in front, but he paid no attention. The snow was falling more and more heavily

and now it seemed almost as if they were flying over the hedges and ditches. Kay was frightened. He tried to pray but could not remember the right words. All he could say was his seven times table.

The snowflakes became larger and larger until they looked like white geese. Suddenly the great sleigh stopped and the driver stood up. It was a *lady*. Her fur and cap were made completely of ice. It was the Snow Queen.

"That was a fine ride," she said. "Come, you are trembling with cold. Creep into my fur." And she put Kay beside her, wrapping the fur round him so that he seemed to sink into a snowdrift. Then she kissed the top of his head. The kiss went straight to his heart, which was already nearly a lump of ice. It now seemed colder than ever.

"My sled!" he cried. "I musn't forget my sled." The sled was tied to the back of one of the white geese which flew behind them. The Snow Queen kissed Kay again and he forgot all about Gerda, the old grandmother and his home.

"Now I shall give you no more kisses," she said, "or I shall kiss you to death."

Kay looked at the Snow Queen. She was beautiful, so beautiful he did not feel in the least afraid. She smiled at him and he told her he could do mental arithmetic, that he knew the names of the main rivers and how many people lived in his country. And she continued to smile. Then it seemed to Kay that what he knew was not enough and he looked up into the black sky where the moon shone cold and bright. They flew over woods and lakes, over forests and hills; below them roared the cold winter wind, the wolves howled and the ice crackled. Kay looked at the long, long winter night. By day he slept at the Snow Queen's side.

The Third Chapter

THE OLD WOMAN AND THE FLOWER GARDEN

But what happened to little Gerda when Kay did not come home? Nobody knew where he had gone. The other boys only said that they saw him tie his little sled to a big white sleigh which had gone out of the town gate. Gerda cried hot tears into her pillow every night: she was sure Kay had been drowned in the river that flowed past their school.

At last spring came with warm sunshine. "Kay is dead," said Gerda.

"No, I am certain he is not," said the sunshine.

"We don't believe he is dead," said the sparrows.

At last Gerda came to be sure that Kay was indeed still alive.

One morning, she said to herself, "I will put on my new red shoes, the ones Kay has never seen, and go down to the river to ask for him."

It was still very early. Gerda kissed the old grandmother, put on her new red shoes and slipped down the stairs and out of the town gate towards the river.

"Have you really taken Kay away from me?" she said. "I will give you my new red shoes if you will give him back." And she took off her shoes and threw them into the river. But they fell close to the shore and the little waves soon left them on the dry land. Gerda thought perhaps she had not thrown her precious

116

shoes far enough so she climbed into a boat that lay close by among the reeds. She went to the far end of the boat and threw her shoes into the water. But the boat had not been tied up properly and with Gerda's rocking it glided away from its mooring.

Gerda quickly realized what had happened and hurried to the other end of the boat again, but before she got there the boat was already out in the stream and drifting away fast. Poor Gerda was very frightened and started to cry, but only the sparrows heard her and they flew alongside, chirping, ''Here we are! Here we are!'' Gerda sat quite still as the boat floated down the stream and her little red shoes floated behind.

The banks on either side were very pretty with flowering trees and sheep and cows, but there was not one person in sight. ''Perhaps the river will take me to Kay,'' she thought. At this she became more cheerful and sat up and looked about her.

After some time, the river passed a large cherry orchard where there was a little house with a thatched roof and red and blue windows. Outside stood two wooden soldiers who held their muskets tightly as Gerda floated past. She called out to them for she thought they were alive, but of course they did not answer. The river carried the boat close to the shore and Gerda called still louder. Out of the house came an old woman leaning on a stick. She was wearing a large velvet hat painted with beautiful flowers.

''You poor child,'' she said. ''What are you doing on the great rolling river?'' And she went to the water's edge, hooked the end of her stick over the boat and drew it to land. Then she lifted Gerda out. Gerda was very glad to be on dry land again, but she was a little scared of the old lady.

''Come and tell me everything,'' said the old woman.

And Gerda told her all that had happened. The old woman shook her head. Then Gerda asked her if she had seen Kay. ''He will come soon,'' the old lady replied. ''But in the meantime you must eat my cherries and look at the flowers in my garden, for they are better than any picture book.'' Then she took Gerda's hand and led her into the house. Inside it was very strange, for the window panes were red and blue and yellow and the rooms shone with many-hued light. On the table was a large dish of cherries and Gerda was allowed to eat as many as she wanted. While she was eating the old woman combed her hair with a magic comb, and as she combed, Gerda gradually forgot Kay. For the old woman was a gentle witch. She was not wicked. She could do a little magic and she wanted to keep Gerda. Next, she went into the garden and pointed her stick at all the rose bushes so that they sank into the ground. She did not want Gerda to be reminded of roses.

Now Gerda was allowed to play in the garden among the

flowers. She ran over the grass between the clumps of flowers and she sniffed the blooms. What wonderful scents there were. Every day she played out there in the sunshine. As she played she learnt the name of every flower, and it seemed to her as though one was missing, but she could not tell which one it was. Then one day she was looking at the old lady's hat with its painted flowers. At the very top was a red rose, for the old lady had forgotten to remove it from her hat when she had removed the roses from the garden.

"Why! You have no roses here!" exclaimed Gerda. She ran out into the garden and searched and searched, but not one could she find. She sat down and wept. Her tears fell just where a rosebush lay buried. And as they fell to the earth the bush came out of the ground covered with flowers. Gerda kissed the lovely roses and immediately remembered Kay and her home.

"Oh! Oh!" she said. "What have I been doing? I set out to look for Kay. Do you know where he is?" she asked the roses. "Do you think he is dead?"

"No," replied the roses. "He is not dead. We have been in the ground where all the dead people are buried. And Kay is not there." Then Gerda went to all the other flowers in the garden asking if they had seen Kay, but none of them knew anything about him at all. So she ran to the far end of the garden where there was a door in the wall. It was locked, but when she pulled, the rusty lock soon broke and she ran out on her bare feet into the wide world.

She ran and ran until she was tired. Then she sat down on a large stone and looked around her. Now she realized that summer was over and autumn had come. "Oh, I have wasted the whole summer!" she cried. For in the beautiful garden it was always summer and flowers bloomed all the year round. She stood up to go on, but she was very tired. Everywhere looked cold and bleak. The leaves were turning yellow and most of the fruits had dropped from the trees. Only the bitter sloes remained. Where was she to go now?

The Fourth Chapter

THE PRINCE AND PRINCESS

Gerda just had to sit down again. Then she saw a great crow hopping across the snow. He stopped and looked at her, nodding his head. "Good day! Good day! Kraa! Kraa!" he said. "Where are you going all alone?" Gerda looked at him sadly and told the crow all that happened to her. "Have you seen Kay?" she finished.

"Perhaps, perhaps," he said.

"Oh, do you think so?" she cried, nearly squeezing the crow to death, she was kissing him so hard.

"Gently, gently," said the crow. "It might be Kay, but he has certainly forgotten all about you, now that he is with his princess."

"Is he living with a princess?" asked Gerda.

"Yes. Now stop talking and listen," replied the crow.

"In the country where we are now lives a princess who is amazingly clever. She has read all the newspapers in the world and forgotten them again, she is so clever. Recently she was sitting on her throne, which is not so much fun as people think, and she began to sing a song 'I'll marry, I'll marry. Why should I tarry?' But she wanted a husband who answered when she spoke to him, not one who simply stood and looked handsome, for that was boring. Then she called her ladies-in-waiting and told them of her plans. 'That's a very good idea,' they all agreed. You may be sure that this is all quite true for my sweetheart flies freely about the castle and she told me herself."

Of course the sweetheart was a crow too.

"At once all the newspapers announced, in a border of hearts with the princess's initials, that the princess had decided to be married. Any good-looking young man who wished should come to the castle to talk to the princess. And the princess would choose for her husband the one who seemed most at home there. I promise you," said the crow, "this is all absolutely true. Young men came pouring in, but not one spoke well enough to please the princess. They were fine when they were out on the streets with their friends, but as soon as they were inside the castle and saw the guards in their uniforms and the footmen in their silver liveries and the great halls with their shining candlesticks they became tongue-tied. And when they were standing in front of the throne on which the princess was sitting, they could do nothing except repeat the last words she had spoken herself. It wasn't until they were outside the gates again that they were able to speak. There was a whole row of them from the town gate to the palace gate. I saw it myself," said the crow.

"But Kay? What about Kay? When did he come?" asked little Gerda.

"Wait, wait," said the crow. "On the third day a young fellow walked up to the gates. He had sparkly eyes and long hair, but his clothes were rather shabby."

"That must be Kay!" cried Gerda.

"And he had a little knapsack on his back," said the crow.

"No, that would have been his sled," said Gerda. "For he took that with him."

"Well, I don't know about that," said the crow. "But what I do know is that when he saw the guards and the footmen he was not in the least put out. He simply nodded to them and said, 'That must be tiring work you have.' Then he walked through the halls with their shining candlesticks, and as he walked his boots squeaked most dreadfully. But he was not at all embarrassed."

"That is definitely Kay!" cried Gerda. "He had new boots on and I've heard them squeak."

"He went boldly in to the princess who was sitting on a pearl as big as a spinning wheel and together they had a conversation with much laughter and merriment. And all the ladies-in-waiting and attendants and footmen and pages were standing proudly and haughtily watching."

"That must be dreadful," said Gerda. "And yet Kay won the hand of the princess?"

"If I wasn't a crow I would have married her myself, even though I have a sweetheart of my own. And my sweetheart says that the young fellow said that he had not come to marry the

princess, only to hear how wise she was. But they certainly liked each other, and that's a fact.''

''Oh, that's definitely Kay,'' cried Gerda. ''He is so clever he knows his seven times table, he can do mental arithmetic and he knows all the main rivers. Please take me to the castle so I can find him.''

''Well, that's easier said than done,'' said the crow. ''How are we to get in?''

''Oh, when Kay knows that I am here,'' said Gerda, ''he'll come out and bring me in himself.''

''Wait for me under that tree,'' said the crow and it flew away.

It was quite late in the evening when the crow returned.

''Kraa! Kraa!'' it said. ''My sweetheart greets you kindly and she sends you this little bread roll from the castle kitchen. There's plenty of food there and you must be hungry. But you cannot possibly get into the castle: you have nothing on your feet and the guards would never allow it. But don't worry, my sweetheart knows a little back staircase that leads up to the princess's bed-room. And she knows where the key is hidden."

The crow led Gerda into the palace garden and they waited under the trees until all the lights in the castle went out. Then they went towards a tower where there was a little door that was slightly ajar. Gerda's heart beat frantically with fear and hope. Oh, if only she could find Kay, how wonderful that would be.

Now they were inside. There was a little lamp burning and in the middle of the floor was the tame crow, cocking her head on one side and looking at Gerda.

"My beloved has told me about you, little lady," it said. "Please take the lamp and we will go immediately."

They climbed the stairs and came into a great hall hung with silks and satins, then they passed through another hall, more rich than the first and then they came to the bedchamber. Here the ceiling was like a great tree with leaves made of glass, and in the middle were two beds, hanging on thick stalks of gold, each of them shaped like a lily. One of them was white and in that lay the princess, and the other was red and in that Gerda hoped to find little Kay. She turned one of the red leaves to one side and saw a brown neck. Surely that was Kay! She called his name and held the lamp close to him. He turned and looked at her. But it was not Kay. Then the princess woke up in her white lily and asked who was there. But Gerda burst into tears and told the whole story and all that the two crows had done for her.

"You poor little thing," said the prince and princess.

The prince got up out of his bed so that Gerda could rest there. "How kind he is," thought Gerda as she lay down to sleep.

The following day she was dressed in fine clothes and the princess asked her if she would like to stay with them in the castle.

But she only asked for a pair of boots and a little carriage and a horse to draw it; then she would drive out into the world to look for Kay.

She was given not only boots but a muff as well, and when she was ready to leave, a coach of pure gold stood waiting at the door. On it, gleaming like a star, was the coat of arms of the prince and princess. Coachmen and footmen stood waiting. The prince and princess themselves helped Gerda into the carriage and the crow, who was now married, was to travel with her for the first three miles. His wife stood watching from the doorway flapping her wings, for travel made her sick. The coach was filled with biscuits and fruit for the journey.

"Goodbye, goodbye!" cried the prince and princess. And Gerda wept to be leaving them. And then after the first three miles the crow, too, said goodbye. He flew up into a tree and beat his black wings in farewell as long as he could still see the coach which shone like sunshine.

The Fifth Chapter

THE LITTLE ROBBER GIRL

They drove on through a thick forest where a band of robbers spied the gleaming coach. "Gold! Gold!" they cried and rushed forward. They seized the horse and killed the coachmen and footmen. Then they dragged little Gerda out of the carriage.

"She's a plump little morsel," said the old robber woman who

had a long beard and shaggy eyebrows that hung down over her eyes. "She's like a little pet lamb. How I shall cherish her!" And she drew out her shining knife.

"Oh! Oh!" screamed the old woman, for her own daughter had bitten her ear. "You wicked brat!" she yelled, for now there was no chance to kill Gerda.

"She's mine!" said the little robber girl. "She shall play with me. She will give me her muff and her dress and she shall sleep in my bed."

And then the little girl bit her mother again, so that the old woman leapt high in the air and all the robbers laughed.

"I want to travel in the coach," said the little robber girl.

She and Gerda sat side by side in the coach and drove deep into the forest. The little robber girl was about as tall as Gerda, but stronger and bigger. She had brown skin and black eyes. She put her arm round Gerda's waist and whispered, "I shan't let them kill you as long as I am not angry with you. Are you a princess?"

"No," replied Gerda. And she told the little robber girl all that had happened to her and how she was looking for Kay.

The little robber girl looked at Gerda seriously and said, "I shan't let them kill you even if I do get angry with you, and then I will kill you myself." Then she put her two hands in Gerda's muff and they drove into the courtyard of the robbers' castle.

The castle was cracked from top to bottom, and ravens and crows flew in and out of the cracks and holes. Huge bulldogs jumped up to greet them as they drove in. In the hall a big fire was burning and the place was filled with smoke which peered under the rafters looking for a way out. A large cauldron of good smelling broth was boiling on the fire.

"You shall sleep with me tonight," said the little robber girl.

They were given a lump of bread and some soup and then went to a corner where rugs and straw were spread. Above them seated on perches were rows of pigeons who all seemed to be sleeping, but who turned their heads when the two girls approached.

"All mine," said the little robber girl, and she seized one of the nearest, holding it by its feet and shaking it so that it flapped its

wings. "Kiss it!" she cried, thrusting it into Gerda's face. "Those two are wood rascals," she said, pointing to two wood pigeons sitting in a hole in the wall behind strips of wood. "I have to keep them well locked up or they would fly away. And here's my love, Baa." And grabbing an antler, she dragged towards her a reindeer that was tied up. He had a copper ring around his neck. "I have to keep him tied up too or he would run away. Every night I tickle him with my knife and that frightens him." She drew out a long knife from a crack in the wall and ran it down the reindeer's neck; he kicked his legs and the little robber girl laughed. Then she lay down and pulled Gerda down beside her.

"Do you have your knife beside you when you are asleep?" asked Gerda, looking anxiously at the long sharp blade.

"I always sleep with my knife. You never know what may happen," replied the robber girl. "Now tell me once more all about Kay and how you came to look for him." So Gerda told the little robber girl the whole story all over again, and above them in their cage the wood pigeons cooed while the other pigeons slept on their perches. The little robber girl put her arm around Gerda's neck, held fast on to her knife in her other hand and slept, but Gerda was too frightened even to close her eyes.

Then the wood pigeons said, "Coo! Coo! We have seen Kay. He was sitting beside the Snow Queen in her carriage which drove by the forest as we lay in our nest. She blew upon the branches and all the nestlings died except for us. Coo! Coo!"

"What did you say!" cried Gerda. "Where was the Snow Queen going? Was Kay going with her?"

"She was probably going to Lapland: there is always snow and ice there. Ask the reindeer. He knows. That is his home."

"It is always covered with snow and ice," said the reindeer. "It is

glorious – miles and miles of frozen waste where one can run free. There the Snow Queen has her summer dwelling, but her castle is closer to the North Pole on a little island.''

''Oh, Kay! When shall I find you?'' cried Gerda.

''Lie still,'' said the robber girl, ''and stop talking or I shall stick my knife in you.''

In the morning Gerda told the robber girl what the wood pigeons had said and the robber girl nodded her head and turned to the reindeer and said, ''Do you know where Lapland is?''

''Of course I do!'' it cried. ''Wasn't I born and brought up there? I ran about in the frozen fields.''

''Now listen to me,'' said the robber girl. ''All the men have gone out. Only my mother is still here. About lunchtime she drinks out of the big bottle and then she has a sleep. While she is asleep I'll do something for you.''

Then she jumped out of bed, ran to her mother and hugged her round the neck and pulled her beard, crying, "Good morning, you old nanny-goat!"

When the mother had gone to sleep after lunch, the robber girl went to the reindeer and said, "I'm going to untie you and let you go free so that you may run to Lapland, but you must carry this little girl to the palace of the Snow Queen where her friend is. You heard what she said last night."

The reindeer leaped in the air for joy. Then the robber girl helped Gerda on to its back and tied her on so that she would not fall off. She even gave her a little cushion for a saddle.

"Here are your fur boots," she said, "but I'm keeping your muff as it's so pretty. Still, you won't be cold. Here are two of my mother's socks – they reach up to your elbows and make fine mittens – now you look just like my ugly old mother!"

And Gerda wept for joy.

"Oh, stop crying. You ought to be happy," said the little robber girl. "Here are two loaves of bread and a ham. Now you won't be hungry." She tied these on to the reindeer's back. Then she opened the door, called in the big dogs, and cut the rope with her sharp knife. "Now run," she said to the reindeer, "and look after the little girl."

Gerda put her hands inside the big socks and said, "Goodbye and thank you."

And the reindeer stretched its legs and ran and ran, through the forest, over rocks and stones and vast frozen wastes. The winter sky was lit with flashing fire.

"Those are my northern lights," said the reindeer. And it ran faster and faster, day and night.

The Sixth Chapter

THE LAPP WOMAN AND THE FINNISH WOMAN

At last they stopped in front of a little hut. It was very small, the roof came right down to the ground and it was only possible to go in and out by crawling on one's stomach. There was no one at home but an old Lapp woman who was cooking fish by the light of an oil lamp. The reindeer told her their story, for Gerda was too cold and exhausted to speak.

"Oh, you poor things," said the old woman. "You have a long way to go yet. You have to run all the way to Finland for that is where the Snow Queen is. I'll write a message on a piece of dried cod, for I have no paper, for you to give to a woman in Finland: she can give you more details than I can."

So when Gerda was warmed and rested the Lapp woman wrote a message on a piece of dried fish, gave the fish to her and told her to take good care of it. Then she tied Gerda on to the reindeer again and the reindeer sprang away. The whole night long, while the northern lights burned in the sky, they travelled over the ice and snow until at last they came to the home of the Finnish woman.

The old Finnish woman lived in a large chimney which was so hot that she went about with almost no clothes on. She loosened Gerda's dress, took off her boots and the long socks belonging to the mother of the little robber girl. Then she laid a piece of ice on the reindeer's head and read the message written on the codfish. She read it three times and when she knew it by heart she took the lid off a pan that was simmering on the fire and popped the fish into the pan, for it would be a shame to waste it.

Now the reindeer told her his story and then he told little Gerda's and the old woman listened, blinking with her clever eyes.

"You have great knowledge," said the reindeer. "You can tie the winds of the world together and if a sailor unties one knot he has a

fair wind, if he unties two knots it blows hard, if he unties the third and fourth knots he has a tempest. Can't you give the little girl something so that she will have the power of twelve strong men to overcome the Snow Queen?"

"A lot of use that would be!" exclaimed the old woman.

She went to a bed and brought out a large rolled-up animal hide. She unrolled it and inside was wonderful writing. Slowly and carefully the old woman read until sweat ran down her face. Then the reindeer begged her to do something for Gerda and Gerda looked at her with her eyes full of tears. The old woman drew the reindeer into a corner and whispered to him and laid a fresh lump of ice on his head.

"Little Kay is definitely at the Snow Queen's palace and thinks it the best place in all the world, but that is because he has a splinter of glass in his eye and a small piece in his heart; until these are out he will never want to leave the Snow Queen and she will keep her power over him," whispered the old woman.

"But can't you give Gerda something that will give her power over all this?" asked the reindeer.

"I can give her nothing that she does not have already. Don't you see how everybody loves her? The power of love is greater than anything else. If Gerda cannot get through to the Snow Queen and take the glass out of little Kay, nobody can. Two miles from here the Snow Queen's garden begins; carry Gerda there and put her down beside a large bush with red berries. Now hurry, and come back here when you have done what I say."

Then the old woman lifted Gerda on to the reindeer which ran off as fast it could.

"My boots! My mittens!" cried Gerda.

The reindeer did not stop, but ran on until it came to the bush

with red berries. There it set Gerda down in the snow, kissed her and ran back to the old woman. Poor Gerda stood there with nothing on her feet and with bare hands in the midst of the bitter cold of Finland.

Gerda went forward as well as she could and as she walked there came towards her a whole crowd of snowflakes. They did not fall from the sky, but ran along the ground, faster and faster. And the nearer they came, the larger they grew. Some of them looked like white bears, others like white porcupines, others like knots made of snakes. They were the Snow Queen's guards.

Gerda began to pray and as she prayed her breath came out of her mouth like smoke. Her breath became thicker and thicker and began to look like little angels who grew larger as soon as they touched the ground. They had helmets on their heads and carried spears in their hands. When Gerda had finished her prayer she was surrounded by a great squadron of white angels who struck the terrible snowflakes with their spears so that they broke into a thousand pieces.

Now Gerda could go on towards the Snow Queen's palace and the angels stroked her hands and feet so that she did not feel the cold.

The Seventh Chapter

THE SNOW QUEEN'S CASTLE AND WHAT HAPPENED THERE

But what was Kay doing all this time? He was certainly not thinking of Gerda and had no idea that she was standing in front of the Snow Queen's palace.

The walls of the palace were made of drifting snow and the doors and windows were made of biting winds. There were more than a hundred halls, all blown together by snow; the whole palace was lit by the northern lights. How empty and bitterly cold it was: there was no fun to be had here. In the middle of one of the halls was a frozen lake and in the middle of the lake sat the Snow Queen when she was at home; she said she was sitting on the mirror of reason.

In one of these halls was Kay. He was playing with slabs of ice and joining them together to make a pattern. It was the icy game of reason. Kay was quite blue with cold, but he did not notice it for the queen had kissed his shudderings away and his heart was now a lump of ice. He believed his game to be of the greatest importance, but this was only because of the piece of glass sticking in his eye. He wanted to make the pieces of ice form a word – the word ETERNITY – but he could never do it.

"If you can do it," the Snow Queen had said, "I will give you the whole world and a new pair of skates." Then she had hurried away to the warm lands. "I shall look into the black pots of the volcanoes and make them white – that will do the grapes and the lemons good," she murmured icily.

So Kay was quite alone in the icy hall when Gerda stepped through the wide doorway. The winds blew their freezing fingers through the palace, but Gerda prayed a little prayer and the winds lay down. When she saw Kay, she ran to him and held him in her arms. "Kay! At last I have found you!"

But Kay sat stiff and cold. Gerda wept hot tears that fell on his chest and went to his heart. They thawed the lump of ice and dissolved the little piece of glass there. He looked at Gerda and she sang a little song to him. Then Kay burst into tears and the splinter of glass came out of his eye. Now he recognized Gerda and cried out: "Gerda! What are you doing here? Where have you been all this time?" Then he looked around him. "How cold it is. And how empty and chilling." They clung to each other and Gerda laughed and wept for joy. It was so wonderful that even the pieces of ice danced for joy. Then they made themselves into the word Eternity – the word the Snow Queen had dared Kay to make.

Then Gerda kissed Kay's cheeks and they were filled with roses, she kissed his eyes and they sparkled like her own, she kissed his hands and they were warm and friendly. The Snow Queen could come home now: the word for his freedom lay there in shining letters of ice.

Then they held each other's hands and stepped out of the palace, talking of home, of the old grandmother and the rose bushes. When they came to the bush with red berries the reindeer was waiting for them with another younger reindeer who gave the children warm milk. Then the two reindeer carried Kay and Gerda first to the old woman in Finland, who gave them instructions for their journey home, and then to the woman in Lapland

who had made them new clothes. The two reindeer accompanied them to the boundary of their country where they said farewell. Now green shoots began to sprout and the birds began to sing and soon the whole forest was covered in green. Out of the forest came a beautiful horse, the same one that had drawn Gerda's carriage, and a young girl came riding up with a red cap on her head and a pair of shining pistols at her side. This was the little robber girl who had grown bored staying at home and decided to travel, first to the north and then wherever her fancy took her. She recognized

Gerda at once and very pleased they were to see each other.

"Well, you're a fine fellow," she said to Kay. "I hope you're worth someone running to the end of the world looking for you." But Gerda smiled and asked after the prince and princess.

"They've gone on their travels," said the robber girl.

"And the crow?" asked Gerda.

"The crow is dead," she answered. "And the other one is now a widow. But tell me about yourself and how you found him in the end."

So Kay and Gerda told their story.

"Snip-snap-snorum!" said the robber girl.

Then she took both their hands and promised that if she should ever come to their town she would pay them a visit. And she rode away into the wide world. But Kay and Gerda went on hand in hand. As they went, spring came with green leaves and flowers and birdsong. Church bells were ringing and they recognized their own town. They went to the grandmother's door and up the stairs to the garret, where everything was just as it had always been. But as they went through the rooms they realized that they had grown up. The roses out on the roof were in flower and there were the little stools. They each sat down on their own stool and held hands. The cold, empty grandeur of the Snow Queen's palace was no more than an ugly dream. The grandmother was sitting in the sunshine and she read aloud, "Except ye become as little children, you shall in no wise enter into the kingdom of God."

Kay and Gerda looked into each other's eyes and understood. And it was summer – warm, glorious summer.